'Why do I have to come?' Joanne asked, between mouthfuls of the lovely crispy bacon.

'Well, Barbara arrived at the front door at some unreasonably early hour this morning. Her eyes almost popped out of her head when I opened the door in my singlet and trousers, and when I asked her to stay while I shopped for some food for our breakfast I thought she was going to have a palsy stroke! I wouldn't let her wake you up. I'm sorry, my dear,' Cam said contritely, the smile behind his eyes belying his words, 'but your reputation is in shreds. There's nothing for it—you're going to have to get out of town.

'But do you want a woman of ill repute as your assistant?' Joanne asked, trying to keep her voice serious.

'I told you,' he shook his head despondently, 'I'm desperate. Scarlet woman or not, the job is yours. Now, eat. I'm off to do the coffee.' And he left her choking on a piece of bacon.

Marion Lennox has had a variety of careers—medical receptionist, computer programmer and teacher. Married, with two young children, she now lives in rural Victoria, Australia. Her wish for an occupation which would allow her to remain at home with her children, her dog and the budgie led her to attempt writing a novel.

Previous Titles

CRUEL COUNTRY
DARE TO LOVE AGAIN

DOCTOR TRANSFORMED

BY

MARION LENNOX

MILLS & BOON LIMITED
ETON HOUSE   18–24 PARADISE ROAD
RICHMOND   SURREY   TW9 1SR

*First published in Great Britain 1991
by Mills & Boon Limited*

© Marion Lennox 1991

*Australian copyright 1991
Philippine copyright 1991
This edition 1991*

ISBN 0 263 77217 9

*Set in 10 on 12 pt Linotron Times
03-9104-51736
Typeset in Great Britain by Centracet, Cambridge
Made and printed in Great Britain*

CHAPTER ONE

THE silver-grey hearse turned into the street behind the hospital, scattering the local children playing hop-scotch on the road. As it drew to a halt the children melted back on to the pavement. They knew a hearse when they saw one, and many of them had heard the news from their parents. Mrs Tynon was dead.

The children were intensely interested. Some were secretly rather pleased, although they wouldn't admit it for fear of hurting Dr Jo. The children liked Dr Joanne Tynon, despite her mother's waving her stick at them and telling them to clear off whenever they ventured too close to the Tynons' front window.

As Joanne thanked the driver for bringing her home the children watched respectfully from a distance. It was not until the car had purred quietly away that Billy, the bravest of the group, ventured to approach.

'We're sorry about your mum, Dr Jo,' he called politely. He wasn't sorry at all, but he didn't like the look on Dr Jo's face and could think of nothing more appropriate to say.

'Thank you, Billy,' Joanne replied with a tired smile. 'I'm sorry we interrupted your game.' She slid the key into the lock of Number Twelve and retreated from their sympathetic eyes.

It was over. She stood with her back against the closed door and the thought filled her, swelling within her until she felt like screaming in an agony of release. Over! Over! Over! The interminable demands were ended. Joanne looked guiltily up the stairs, half expecting the querulous voice to come floating down.

'Joanne, you're late. When are you going to get my tea?'

Every night for the past twenty years Joanne had listened to that same demand. Coming home from another funeral twenty years ago, as a bereft, frightened eight-year-old, shattered by the loss of her gentle father, Joanne had watched her mother go up those stairs with the order, 'Get me some tea.' The demands had been constant ever since.

Joanne walked into the dingy front room and sat listlessly on the settee. She kicked off her sensible brown shoes and stared at them in dislike. She hated them. She hated this room. It was caught in a time warp. Nothing had changed since her father's death.

She was caught in the same warp. Her mother had allowed nothing to change. Every move by Joanne to bring some change to the house, some life, had brought on her palpitations.

Mostly Joanne hadn't tried to fight. She had learned early that it wasn't worth the fuss. As a little girl she had submitted to the dreary, out-of-date clothes. As she had gradually learned to accept the taunts of her classmates, her clothes had ceased to be important.

She stood up and looked in the gilt-edged mirror on the wall. If it weren't for the flawless complexion and willow-slim figure she could be taken for forty. Her tweed suit was outdated and severe; her hair was pulled back in an unbecoming knot. Forty! She was twenty-eight, and she felt about a hundred.

Joanne's father had been a doctor at the hospital over the road. Her mother had therefore deemed it suitable for Joanne to stay at school and then study medicine at the university near the hospital. It had suited Joanne. With no social life to speak of, she had immersed herself in the medicine her father had loved, drawing solace from its heavy workload. It was one way she could avoid the shrill-voiced criticism and incessant demands of her mother.

Joanne had stayed at the same hospital, first to do her residency and then taking a permanent job as medical officer in Casualty. While she worked there she had had the sense of marking time. She couldn't stay in the one hospital all her life.

Finally she had come to a decision: she didn't want to be a specialist. She loved treating the wide variety of patients who streamed through the hospital casualty department, and had come to the conclusion that she was going to try general practice. It would involve a move.

Telling her mother had been one of the heardest things Joanne had ever had to do. It had proved worse than she had feared. Her mother's fury had brought on palpitations, and finally the heart attack she had been threatening Joanne with for so many years.

And now she was dead. Buried, with no one in attendance except a dry-eyed daughter whose only feeling was one of numb, cold relief. Guilt? Perhaps a little, but she could live with the thought that her mother's rage had killed her. Her mother's death had been the spectre used to frighten a little girl into submission. Now that it had finally happened it meant only relief.

Joanne shook her head, sorrow pervading her at the thought of the wasted, bitter life.

And now? She was lost, like a beetle who, having

spent all his life under a brick, had suddenly had the brick lifted. The world was exposed. What now?

She wasn't going to stay here. She glared around the room as if it had a life of its own—at the hideous purple curtains, dark brown furniture, faded mauve lampshade. She reached down and picked up one of the sensible shoes and hurled it with all her might at the hated lamp. It shattered, smashing into a thousand pieces. Joanne slumped back into a chair, burying her face in her hands. Unnoticed by her, a dumpy figure appeared at the door and stood watching sympathetically.

'Can I join in, or is this a private war?'

Joanne raised her eyes. It was her friend Barbara. Joanne stared at her speechlessly, then burst into tears.

Barbara dropped clumsily to her knees—at eight months pregnant no easy feat—and held her until the worst had passed.

'I knew you should have let me come,' she said crossly, as Joanne finally subsided.

Joanne groped for a handkerchief and blew her nose decisively. 'It would have been stupid. She disliked you, and the feeling was mutual.'

'You're right there,' Barbara admitted. 'And if you're honest with yourself, you felt the same.'

Barbara had been around for almost as long as Joanne could remember. She had been a school friend, cheerfully latching on and protecting the waif-like Joanne as they passed through school and university. She had accepted Mrs Tynon's vitriol with equanimity, braving it when necessary in order to continue her friendship with Joanne. Married to a surgeon, she had put her own medical career on the back boiler and was devoting herself to her husband, to the bump, as she called her impending baby, and to 'doing something about Joanne'. Now she took Joanne's hands and gripped them hard.

'Guess what? I've found you a job!'

Joanne looked up at her friend, surprised out of her misery.

'It's true,' Barbara continued. 'Now, I'll make us a nice cup of tea, you retrieve your shoe from that lot,' she indicated the mound of shattered glass, 'and I'll take you for an interview.'

'But I don't want a job.'

Barbara stood up awkwardly and pulled Joanne after her. 'Yes, you do,' she said kindly. 'You said so last week.'

'But that was before. . .'

'Yes, I know,' Barbara said firmly. 'Before your mother died. Don't you dare let her stop you even now. She's dead, Joanne, and you have to get away from here. Good grief, look at you! You've been cooped up here with your dragon of a mother all your life and it's time you got out, to see what the big bad world is all about.'

Joanne smiled faintly and looked around again. 'I don't know. Probably you're right. There's a lot to be sorted out here, though, before I can think of moving.' The thought of staying much longer in the dreary little house chilled her to the bone.

'No,' Barbara grabbed her by the shoulders and shook her excitedly, 'I can do better than that. I've thought it all out over lunch, and it's all organised.'

'All organised,' Joanne repeated, bemused.

'Yes, and I won't take no for an answer,' her friend said belligerently. 'Wayne brought a friend home for lunch. He's a surgeon in charge of the hospital at

Strathleath Island and he's looking for an assistant. How about that?' She stood back, waiting for a reaction.

'Strathleath Island!' Joanne looked up, faintly stunned. 'That's off the coast of Queensland, isn't it?'

'Oh, Joanne, for heaven's sake!' Barbara expostulated. 'Of course you know it. It's one of the islands off the Great Barrier Reef. Wayne and I went there for our honeymoon, and it's fabulous. There's a ferry across from the mainland, or it takes about fifteen minutes by plane. It has a small town and a jetty and a fishing fleet, but the rest is just mountains, bush and miles and miles of glorious beaches. Joanne, I'd kill to live there! It's the chance of a lifetime.'

'You can't be serious?'

'Never more so. Look.' Barbara reached out and gripped Joanne's arms, her eyes growing intense. 'Everyone knows you here. You've got a nice little mould for yourself as quiet, shy, drab Joanne Tynon, who never agrees to any social life and never has any fun. You've got to go where you can break out of this awful mould before. . .' her eyes took in Joanne from head to foot '. . .before you turn into what you look.'

'Thanks a lot.' Joanne tried to sound indignant, but it didn't quite come off. She knew Barbara was speaking no more than the truth.

Barbara laughed. 'Oh, I know I should shut up. Wayne always says I step in where angels fear to tread. But this is perfect. And I wouldn't mind working with Cameron Maddon myself. At least come and meet him.'

'Now?'

'Yes.' Barbara was almost jumping up and down with excitement, and Joanne burst into laughter.

'Cut it out, or you'll have your baby on the living-room floor! Barbara, be serious. I can't just up and leave.'

'Yes, you can!' Barbara's voice was almost a squeak. 'I said I thought it all out. Wayne and I are desperate to get out of the hospital flat before the baby is born, and we've looked and looked. We, kindest, dearest Joanne, could look after your house for you while you're off seeing the world.'

Joanne stared at her, dumbfounded, and Barbara grasped her hands.

'I know, I know—it's much too soon. Wayne told me so at lunchtime and said I wasn't to push you, but it does seem so perfect. Cam is desperate for help, you're desperate for a change and we're desperate for a house.'

Joanne stared at her again and then round at the dreary room. 'But it's dreadful. You'd hate it,' she said softly. 'I hate it.'

Barbara shook her head. 'It hasn't been my prison for the last twenty years as it's been for you.' She gazed around her thoughtfully. 'If you let me have my head I could make it a lovely, cheerful home for Wayne and me and the bump. Then, if you want to reclaim it when you're done with wandering, it'll still be here waiting for you.'

Joanne shook her head. 'You'd better stop—you're making me dizzy.'

'OK, OK. But you'll come and meet him?'

'But. . .' Joanne stopped helplessly, then asked in spite of herself, 'What's he like?'

Barbara grinned. 'I thought you'd never ask. He's gorgeous.'

'Barbara!'

The other girl held up her hands. 'I know, I know—that's not what you're interested in. It ought to be, but you've blocked it out of your life since you realised your mother was going to come between you and any male remotely interesting.' She ignored Joanne's attempt at protest and continued.

'He's Wayne's age, in his mid-thirties. He went through medical school with Wayne and then decided to do surgery in England. He did brilliantly at surgery, and I gather didn't do too badly in his private life either. When Wayne knew him there was always a string of beautiful women in tow. He finally married one—Wayne flew over to be best man at his wedding about six years ago. Lindy was an actress, and the way Wayne raved when he returned had me feeling inferior for weeks. Apparently she was stunning. Something went wrong, though, and the next thing we heard Cam had set up practice on Strathleath and Lindy was still in England.' She paused for breath, then, as Joanne still looked bemused, she continued.

'Cam's had a succession of assistants. The last one married and is due to have a baby about the same time I am, so he's wanting someone in a hurry. He sat over lunch and itemised every quality he wanted in an assistant until I thought I'd burst. You fit every one.'

'Do you think so?'

'I know.' Barbara held up a hand and counted fingers. 'You're young, fit and enthusiastic. You're sober, hard-working and dedicated.' She flashed a grin at Joanne and went back to her fingers. 'You're not a flibbertigibbet.' She giggled. 'I gather the last one was. He doesn't sound at all impressed by his last assistant—he says all she was interested in was her appearance and her love life.' She stared again at her fingers, remembering. 'You've got solid training in anaesthetics and obstetrics and,' she ended triumphantly, 'you finish up here in a fortnight and are free to leave.'

Joanne stared at her, her mind in a whirl. Could she? It would be crazy to go in such a rush, to somewhere she had only vaguely heard of. Strathleath Island. She knew the name, nothing else.

'It really is a beautiful place to live,' Barbara broke into her train of thought. She had always known what Joanne was thinking. It was one of the reasons they were still friends. As Mrs Tynon had thrown more and more obstacles in the path of their friendship and Joanne had gone on politely declining Barbara's friendly invitations, Barbara had been able to read the desperate loneliness behind the polite façade. 'A tropical paradise, Joanne.' She sounded almost pleading.

'OK,' Joanne held up her hands, 'I know when I'm beaten. I'll meet this man. Mind,' she added hastily as Barbara's face creased in delight, 'I'm doing no more than finding out about it. Cameron Maddon might be offering tuppence-halfpenny a week as wages and every fourth Sunday afternoon off if I've been good. But,' she smiled gently at her friend, 'I'll find out.'

'Now.'

'For heaven's sake!' Joanne shook her head. 'I can't now. Organise it for tomorrow morning. I look. . .' She gazed down at herself with the same dislike she had shown as she had gazed at the mauve lamp. Not that she had anything better to put on. And how could she be interviewed feeling the way she did at the moment, caught in a haze of shock and unreality?

'You look serious,' Barbara assured her. She reached out and touched Joanne's cheek. 'And exhausted, poor lamb. You've had a rotten few days. But Cam goes back tomorrow—he only dropped in to see Wayne on the last day of a conference here. Besides. . .' She broke off, not knowing quite what to say without giving undue offence to Joanne. The impression Barbara had received was that Cameron Maddon had little time for women who dressed to attract. Barbara had her own ideas about that—but first to get Joanne to the interview. 'Oh, come on, Joanne,' she begged. 'It's worth a try.'

Joanne flung her hands up helplessly. After all, there could be no harm in meeting the man. And perhaps. . . She looked around once more at the brown walls closing in on her. Perhaps she was better walking out on this part of her life where the haunting echoes of her mother's voice still pervaded.

CHAPTER TWO

JOANNE entered the hospital with a feeling of unreality. She had not been at work since her mother's death two days ago. She felt different. Her life had changed dramatically, and yet here was a world where everything looked and sounded the same as before. She walked in through the Casualty entrance, and the nursing staff and orderlies greeted her with real sympathy, adding to her sense of unreality. She had an urge to bolt home, don her white coat and come back ready to immerse herself in her work. At least then the patients would treat her as normal. By the look of the number of patients waiting to be seen, she was being missed. Barbara was with her, however, and dragged her inexorably on.

They made their way through the wide corridors to the surgeons' consulting-rooms. Wayne and his friend were deep in conversation, and looked up in surprise as Barbara knocked and entered, ushering Joanne before her.

'Joanne!' Wayne rose, a short, balding man with kindly eyes and a warm smile. 'Did you let Barbara drag you here? Really, Barbara, you go too far.' He came across the room to give Joanne a quick hug, at the same time glaring at his wife. That lady looked remarkably unperturbed.

'It was the only way they were going to meet,' Barbara responded calmly. 'And you have to admit it would be a shame for Joanne to miss the opportunity if Cam thinks she's suitable.'

'There's always application forms and the postal services,' Wayne said severely. 'You had no right to interrupt Jo this afternoon.'

'Should you be working?' The soft words came from the other side of the room, and Joanne turned from Wayne's encircling arm to meet Cameron Maddon.

Her first impression of Cam Maddon was of size. As he rose he towered over the others in the room. Dark eyes were set deeply into his tanned face. His jet-black hair and his thick dark eyebrows shaded his face to make it seem as if he was surveying the world from shadow. It was a strong face, thought Joanne. His mouth was curved in a faint smile, but in his eyes she read disapproval. Of what? Of the thought of her dropping urgent work to grab a chance at a job interview? Obviously neither Wayne nor Barbara had told him why she was free this afternoon. She flushed.

'No, I'm not working this afternoon,' she responded calmly. 'As Barbara said, it seemed a good idea to find out about a job which may be suitable.'

He frowned as if not totally convinced but came forward to be introduced. Goodness, he was big! Joanne's hand was taken in a strong grip. She looked up at his face, aware of intensive scrutiny.

'Joanne Tynon. Wasn't there a Tynon who was a surgeon here? There's a Tynon Wing named after him.'

'My father,' Joanne agreed. 'He died twenty years ago.'

Cameron furrowed the heavy brows in an effort of remembering. 'I can recall my professor of surgery talking of his achievements. Techniques he pioneered in heart surgery are still in use today. Do you take after him?'

The question caught Joanne unprepared and she grimaced. Her mother had pushed her in every way she knew to replace her dead father, and comparisons touched a raw nerve.

'I'm told I look like him a little,' she answered softly. 'I'm not interested in surgery as a career, though.'

'Because of the comparison?'

Joanne met his gaze squarely. 'No. I've thought that one out, and it's not true. I prefer the aches and pains of general practice.'

He smiled, his intense face lighting.

Joanne could sense the beginning of approval. His wary manner relaxed. Wayne was called back to the wards and ushered Barbara out with him. As they left, Cam motioned towards a chair and reseated himself.

'OK, Joanne Tynon, tell me about yourself.'

He proceeded to throw question after question at her, probing her training, knowledge and experience. Her replies obviously pleased him. She knew her background would be right for an assistantship such as he was offering and was quietly confident of her medical capabilities, and it must have shown.

For the first time she acknowledged to herself that this job had possibilities. The man interviewing her, she was sure, was over-qualified for the position he held and would be a strong medical partner.

As the questions drew to a close, Cam seemed to come to a decision and started to outline the job in detail. The hospital was small but magnificently equipped, as the two doctors on the island had to be able to deal with every emergency. Small planes could be used to transfer patients to the large hospital at

Cairns, but this was not possible in bad weather. In the cyclone season they were often isolated for days at a time.

Cam's voice was deep and resonant. Relaxed in an armchair in Wayne's office, he kept his gaze fixed firmly on Joanne as he spoke. Despite the awful day she had so far endured, Joanne felt her lethargy lift and the interest in the job stir within her. Cam Maddon presented as a competent professional who knew his job and believed in what he was doing. What Joanne was still unsure of in general practice she felt sure he would be able to teach her.

As he talked she found herself wondering what sort of man he was. One of her initial impressions of him had been wariness, and she wondered why. She looked across at the tall, dark figure lounging back in the armchair. He possessed strength. It was contained, disguised by the beautifully tailored suit, but Joanne felt with certainty that beneath the manicured exterior lay a hard, muscled body. Hard. She felt around the adjective cautiously and finally deemed it appropriate. He was charming now, Joanne thought, but that was because he had decided she was suitable for the job and wanted her to accept. There was little Cam Maddon wanted that he wouldn't be able to get, she thought.

The effect of the long morning started to seep back, and she found her attention wandering. She felt strange and out of place. The emotions of the last few days were still too strong to let her go for more than a few moments. Suddenly the need to be alone was overpowering. She stood up, smoothing down the hated tweed skirt.

'Do I take it I'm suitable for the job?' she asked brusquely.

Cam Maddon stood also, his thick brows creased in surprise. Clearly he wasn't used to being cut short.

'I think you may be, Dr Tynon. I need time to consider. Have you no questions yourself?'

'Not that I can think of now,' Joanne replied shortly. 'I'll ring you when I've had time to think it through.'

'Why do you need to rush off? There are probably more things you should know if you seriously want to consider the position.'

'I've things to attend to,' she replied briefly. The heat of the room was closing in on her and a nerve at the back of her eyes was beginning to throb.

'But you're not working.' His eyes once again perused her drearily clad figure. 'I'm keeping you from social engagements?'

It was a question. Joanne gazed blankly at the man in front of her. The faint derision in his tone was an insult. Obviously he could not see what could be more urgent than discussion of a future career. Joanne still had to cope with an interview with her mother's lawyer, however, and she had had enough. To her horror she felt the pricking of tears behind her aching eyes. Damn the man for his probing arrogance! She caught herself and tried to keep her voice firm.

'As you say. Now, if you'll excuse me. Perhaps you could phone me with other details we need to finalise. If you decide you want me Wayne will give you my number.'

She looked up and caught the dark eyes staring in puzzlement and something else. Concern? She met his look briefly and tried to dredge up a smile, then turned and fled.

* * *

Wayne brushed past her as he returned to his rooms, but Joanne didn't notice. He turned and watched as she retreated down the corridor, then entered his rooms to find his friend with a bemused expression on his face.

'Well?'

Cam looked up. 'Oh, Wayne. Look, I'll get out of your way. It was good of you to let me use your rooms.'

Wayne waved his thanks aside. 'It's OK—I'm not seeing patients this afternoon. Tell me, what did you think of our Joanne?'

Cam's face creased in perplexity. 'She certainly seems medically competent. She has the qualifications and experience I'm looking for. What's eating her, though?'

'Sorry?'

'She's as edgy as a rabbit, and I thought she was crying at the end of the interview. The last thing I want is an assistant with emotional problems.'

Wayne's lips tightened and he looked appraisingly at the other man. 'Did she give you a reason?'

'I didn't ask,' Cam said shortly. 'Her answers to my questions were all satisfactory, but as soon as I'd finished she cut me short. Obviously she had much more pressing ways of spending her time. Perhaps I'd be better off holding out for a male for the job.'

There was a biting edge to his tone, and Wayne regarded his friend curiously. He had certainly learned to judge women harshly.

'I think you'd find any male would be just as tense in the same circumstances,' he commented drily. 'Joanne's mother was buried this morning—that's why she had the day off.'

Cam stared at him for a drawn-out moment and then let out an expletive. 'Why the hell didn't you tell me?'

'I didn't have time,' Wayne defended himself. 'I'm sorry, but I didn't expect Barbara to spring her on us like that. I trust it hasn't made a difference?'

Cam shook his head thoughtfully. 'No. Apart from putting my foot in it and possibly alienating her from the thought of working with me, that is. I take it she's normally much calmer?'

'Much calmer,' Wayne agreed quietly.

'I must admit I was favourably impressed,' Cam continued. 'It's a refreshing change to meet a woman who doesn't dress to attract.'

Wayne raised his eyebrows in exaggerated disbelief, and Cam gave a short, mirthless laugh.

'Oh, yes, I'd forgotten you'd met Lindy. I remember you were bowled over just like I was.'

'Well, not quite,' Wayne laughed. 'I was already safely married to Barbara at the time. She was a knock-out, all the same.' He paused, looking up at his friend's tightened expression before continuing gently, 'Do you want to tell me what went wrong?'

For a moment he thought Cam wasn't going to answer. The silence stretched out.

'I'm sorry,' Wayne said finally. 'It's none of my business. Forgive me for asking.'

Cam shook his head. 'Don't be sorry. I don't talk about it if I can help, but I shouldn't block friends out. I've been doing too much of that.'

'By moving to Strathleath Island?'

Cam nodded. 'I just wanted to get away. I was so sick with myself for being taken in.' He paused and then continued decisively, 'You're right—Lindy was beautiful. Everything about her was beautiful—her looks, her laugh, her voice. She had the knack of making any person she talked to feel as if they were the only important person in the world. I met her when I was at a low ebb. My father had just died over here while I was away in England, and I was questioning what the hell I was doing concentrating on a career when my family needed me. Lindy picked me up and soothed me, built up my ego again. I thought I was the luckiest man alive when she agreed to marry me.'

'And?' Wayne probed gently.

Cam turned and looked bleakly out of the window at the slow-moving traffic below. 'I was important to Lindy when she met me,' he replied eventually. 'Her acting career hadn't taken off at that time, and she saw me as a secure financial base to support her while she launched her career.'

Wayne said nothing, and the silence hung between them. Finally Cam shrugged and went on, 'I guess there's not very much to tell. At the same time as I started to pressure Lindy to ease up on a career that was taking her away from home for ninety per cent of the time she met someone who could offer her far more than I had. End of story.'

CHAPTER THREE

WHETHER to accept the job with Cam Maddon was only one of a thousand thoughts whirling in Joanne's head as she tried to sleep that night.

Her head was still throbbing. Late that afternoon she had spent an hour with her mother's lawyer and had left feeling stunned. Joanne had always been told they were poor. That fact was so blatantly untrue that the lawyer's figures had made her feel faint. She thought back to the times she had gone without, birthday parties she hadn't gone to as a little girl because there was never enough money for a dress, and the demands her mother had made as soon as Joanne started earning money. She had known nothing but dreary poverty, Joanne thought bitterly as she tossed restlessly in the hard bed, and for what? Her father had left them comfortably off. The lawyer's astute investments and her mother's parsimony had left her wealthy.

She was bone-weary, but sleep would not come. Finally she rose and crossed to the window. It was still early. Outside the street was alive with traffic as hospital visitors searched for parking places in the back streets. As Joanne watched, a taxi drew to a halt outside her little house, and with a shock she recognised the tall figure emerging. Cam Maddon.

She glanced at her bedroom clock. It was only eight p.m. With little sleep on the previous few nights she had gone to bed early, and this was the price. It wasn't an unreasonable time to call. She grimaced, the ache behind her eyes intensifying. There was no time to dress or knot her hair. As the doorbell rang she reached for the drab dressing-gown behind the door and hurried down the stairs.

'Good evening.' Cam sounded slightly amused as she cautiously opened the door to the width of the safety chain. 'Have I got you out of bed?'

'Yes.'

'Can I come in?'

She stared at him and then pulled herself together. Lifting the chain off the hook, she ushered him into the front room. As she flicked on the light she was miserably aware of the dinginess of the room. She and her mother had had so few visitors she had ceased to consider it important, especially as she had been told repeatedly that there was no money for refurbishing. Glass from the shattered light still lay on the carpet. Cam raised his eyebrows, but said nothing.

'What can I do for you?' Joanne fought to keep the nervousness from her voice.

'I came to apologise.'

'Apologise?' She was startled.

'For my boorish behaviour this afternoon. After you'd gone Wayne explained why you were on edge and upset. My behaviour was unforgivable, and I'm sorry.' He smiled down at her as he spoke, and Joanne found herself responding to the quiet warmth behind his eyes.

'You weren't to know.'

'No. But I made assumptions that were incorrect, and I'm sorry.' His eyes held hers reassuringly. 'Are you here by yourself?'

'Yes.' Her reply was defensive.

'Well, you shouldn't be. Haven't you any family?'

Joanne tried vainly to put off her sense of unreality and put some sort of assurance into her voice. 'I'm fine, thank you, Mr Maddon. I'm just tired. If you'll excuse me. . .' If he didn't go soon, she thought, she was going to fall over. She felt dizzy and sick.

'When did you last eat?'

She looked at him blankly.

'Oh, for heaven's sake! You look as if you're about to pass out. Did you eat dinner?' Then, as she continued to look speechlessly at him, he nodded. 'I thought not. And what about lunch?'

'Barbara made me a cup of tea,' she said defensively, and he snorted derisively.

'Great. Where's the kitchen?' Then, as he realised Joanne was too stunned to speak, he wheeled and disappeared into the back of the house. Two minutes later he was back.

'What sort of place is this? For heaven's sake, there's not even a lettuce leaf in the refrigerator!'

'There's cereal and milk,' Joanne replied defensively.

'Terrific. You don't need breakfast, Dr Tynon. You need dinner.'

'I'm fine,' she protested. 'Really. I'm just very tired. I've had very little sleep over the past few nights.'

'You're not able to sleep, though, are you?' he demanded. His voice gentled. 'Look, I've lost my parents too, and I know how it feels.'

'I can look after myself, thank you.' Joanne flung the retort at him, aware of its rudeness but unable to prevent it. She didn't need sympathy; it made her feel like a fraud.

'I'm sorry, but you're going to have to accept.' The

lazy smile had returned. 'Just regard it as pure self-interest on my part. I don't want my future assistant fainting by the wayside or suffering a decline before I can get my two bob's worth of work out of her.' He gave her a long, hard look as if defying her to argue, but Joanne was past arguing. She shook her head numbly, a gesture he ignored.

'I noticed a take-away food place at the end of the street. I'll be back in ten minutes with hamburgers for two. If this place runs to it, which I must confess to doubting, see if you can dredge up two plates and a couple of glasses.'

He was gone, with Joanne left standing stupidly in the middle of the room. She wasn't sure whether to laugh or to cry. In the end she did neither. Her mind was no longer functioning. Mechanically, she used the time he was gone to sweep up and dispose of the shattered glass and set the kitchen table.

He returned before she had finished, bearing steaming hamburgers crammed to bursting-point with 'the lot', a newspaper-wrapped parcel of crisp golden chips and a bottle of wine. Joanne was pushed unceremoniously into a chair while Cam served out the food.

'Now eat,' he ordered.

'You sound just like Barbara,' Joanne smiled faintly. 'Bossy.'

He laughed easily. 'Yes, I'm sure Wayne is kept nicely under the thumb.' He bit into his hamburger, keeping his eyes on her as he ate. 'Tell me, is Barbara putting pressure on you to take this job? It seems to me you're being bulldozed a bit.'

'Don't you want me?'

'I didn't say that.' A slow smile lit the darkness of his face. 'It's just that I've now had time to talk to

Wayne and he's told me how much Barbara would like this house.' His look as he perused the room told her that he couldn't understand it, but he continued. 'I know you're her friend. Are you considering the job because of that?'

'No.' Joanne forced herself to speak with difficulty. 'I was planning a move anyway, before. . .before my mother died.'

'Taking her with you?'

'No.' Joanne looked up at him and then down to the plate of food in front of her. 'No. She wouldn't have moved. My mother was supportive of my medicine, supportive of me only as long as I stayed in this house and at my father's hospital.'

There was a long pause.

'You had an argument about it?'

Joanne gave a bitter laugh. 'You could say that.'

'And she died.'

'Yes.' She swallowed a mouthful of her bun without tasting it. 'She always said she would if I crossed her, and she did.' She raised her hamburger to her mouth again but couldn't bring herself to bite. The choking anger rose again, engulfing her in misery.

'Oh, my dear, I am sorry.'

Joanne's lips tightened. 'Don't be.' She picked up the uneaten plate of food and crossed to the sink. With her back to him she continued, her voice controlled and even, 'It's got nothing to do with you. My mother was a selfish, manipulative woman.' The control broke suddenly without warning. 'I hated her. Hated her! I'm glad she's dead. Don't feel sorry for me, I can't stand it.'

The plate slipped from her fingers and clattered harmlessly on to the draining-board. She stood staring sightlessly at the spilt food, tears coursing down her cheeks. What he must think of her! Why didn't he go and leave her be?

He was behind her. His hands fell gently on to her shoulders. Joanne stiffened, but the hands ignored her resistance. Firmly she was turned around. Cam stood looking down at the drawn face, grief and strain clearly etched. Joanne made a last attempt to check the tears, but she was past control, past caring what this man thought of her. As he pulled her against him she finally gave in to the torrent of emotion which had been welling in her for the past few days. She buried her face in the roughness of his sweater and allowed herself to be comforted like a lost, hurt child, grateful only for the warmth and comfort of another human being.

The arms held her until the racking sobs subsided. As they eased, a hand went up and softly ran through the fine strands of hair streaming down her back, stroking, caressing. Finally she was limp against him, exhausted of emotion.

'I'll ring Barbara,' he said finally as he felt her stir against him, attempting to rouse herself from the awful lethargy she was left with. 'You're not staying by yourself tonight.'

Joanne shook her head weakly. 'No, that would be stupid. Barbara is eight months pregnant and needs her own bed. Besides,' she attempted a smile, 'with luck she'd have the baby tonight and I'd be up all night again.'

'Well,' Cam looked down at her consideringly, 'there's no help for it, then. You'll have to put up with yours truly.'

She gaped at him. 'You can't stay here.'

'Try and stop me.' Without waiting for a response he

swung her up into his arms. 'You, Dr Tynon, are going to bed. I am going to spend the night on that exceedingly enticing sofa in your front room.'

'But it's as hard as nails.' The thought of her mother's bed flashed through her mind, to be instantly rejected. No.

He was watching her, almost as if he were reading her thoughts. 'I was hoping you weren't going to tell me it was uncomfortable,' he said mournfully. 'How am I going to psych myself into believing I'm sleeping in the lap of luxury now?'

'You can't sleep there.'

'Dr Tynon, do you want this job at Strathleath Island or not?'

'I. . .' Confused, she shook her head at him. 'I don't know. I think I do.'

'Then,' his grip tightened on her, 'learn not to argue with your boss.' Still holding her in his arms, he reached down and retrieved the bottle of wine and a glass.

'You're going to drop something,' Joanne warned.

'Just cross your fingers it's not you.' He grinned down at her, kicking the door open and striding through to the hall.

At the top of the stairs he stopped and raised his brows in a question, and Joanne gestured towards her bedroom door. As he entered he stopped short in amazement.

'You don't sleep in here?'

'Of course I do.' Her voice was defensive.

'It's like something out of *Jane Eyre*! That's a child's bed and, by the look of it, a damned uncomfortable one at that.' He gestured towards the narrow bed in the corner.

Joanne closed her eyes wearily and he looked down at her.

'No questions tonight? OK.' He deposited her on the pulled-back bed and started undoing the buttons of her robe.

'I can do it.'

'Fine, Dr Tynon. You do it.' His voice held amusement and he turned away to pour a glass of wine. When he turned back she was under the covers with the blankets pulled up to hide the scantiness of her nightgown. 'OK. You may have knocked back my food, but you're compelled to drink my wine. One glass for the sake of a good night's sleep.' He stood over her as she drank.

'I spoiled your dinner,' Joanne said ruefully. 'It'll be cold and horrid by now.'

'Yours might be,' he smiled, 'not mine. I have a very strong sense of self-preservation which stands me in good stead in times like these. While you were working yourself up to a fine old storm I was concentrating on the important things in life, such as polishing off my hamburger. Now,' he took her empty glass from her hand, 'you, Dr Tynon, are going to sleep. If you need anything, just call. I'll be directly below.'

'You can't sleep there,' Joanne protested again, but without conviction.

'You're probably right,' he agreed gravely. 'However, if you can sleep in that,' he gestured disdainfully towards her bed, 'then you're setting a challenge that a macho male like me can't resist. I can hardly complain about a little horsehair.' He placed a finger on her lips to quell further protest. 'It'll be good for my soul, like cod liver oil and oat bran.' He smiled down at her.

'Now, no more arguments. Sleep.' He pushed her head down on the pillow and left the room.

Joanne did sleep. The kaleidoscope of thought grew fuzzy and faded into the dark. She knew she should not allow him to stay, but overriding her discomfort at his gesture was the warmth and security of his presence. As she drifted towards sleep the thought of him in the room below was like a solid barrier against the awful loneliness, pain and bitterness of the past few days.

Joanne woke to the smell of bacon. She opened one eye and investigated. On her bedside table was a large plate, buried under a load of eggs, bacon, grilled tomato and toast. As light flooded the room both eyes opened. Cam was pulling wide the curtains, allowing the weak winter sun to penetrate.

'It was true,' she said stupidly. 'You did stay. I thought it was a dream.'

'A nightmare, more like,' he said kindly. 'I'm sorry to have to wake you, but I'm afraid I have a plane to catch and I was determined to see you had at least one decent meal before I left.'

'Oh, no!' she said guiltily. 'I'm so sorry. You shouldn't have stayed.'

'True,' he agreed gravely. 'It has had one good result, though.'

'Which is?'

'I've got myself an assistant. You have to come now.' As she struggled to sit up he handed her a glass of orange juice and watched sternly as she drank. 'Every drop!'

'Yes, sir.' In fact Joanne didn't need forcing. The smell of the food had rekindled her appetite with a vengeance. As she finished her juice he placed the plate of food in front of her and watched with satisfaction as she ate. 'Why do I have to come?' she asked, between mouthfuls of the lovely crispy bacon.

'Well, Barbara arrived at the front door at some unreasonably early hour this morning. Her eyes almost popped out of her head when I opened the door in my singlet and trousers, and when I asked her to stay while I shopped for some food for our breakfast I thought she was going to have a palsy stroke! I wouldn't let her wake you up. I'm sorry, my dear,' he said contritely, the smile behind his eyes belying his words, 'but your reputation is in shreds. There's nothing for it—you're going to have to get out of town.'

'But do you want a woman of ill repute as your assistant?' Joanne asked, trying to keep her voice serious.

'I told you,' he shook his head despondently, 'I'm desperate. Scarlet woman or not, the job is yours. Now, eat. I'm off to do the coffee.' He left her choking on a piece of bacon.

Joanne finished her meal and lay back against the pillows, watching the dappled sunlight ripple on the bedcover. She glanced at the clock on the bedside table. Ten-thirty. She had more than slept the clock around.

The awful oppression had lifted, and it wasn't just the lessening of weariness. Somehow, Cam Maddon had given her the strength to start again, to face a life where decisions were hers to be made.

He came in again bearing hot, fragrant coffee and placed it on the table beside her.

'I have to go.' He stood for a moment staring down at the slight figure in the bed. 'I'd like to formally offer you the job as my assistant, Dr Tynon. Will you accept?'

She looked up at him almost shyly. 'Yes, please, Mr Maddon, I would be very pleased to accept.'

'My name's Cam.'

'And I'm Joanne, please.'

'Fine.' Still he didn't move. Then he bent suddenly and, cupping her chin in his palm, tilted her face upward to kiss her softly on the mouth. The kiss lingered, as if each had found something they didn't quite understand but were reluctant to lose. As they finally drew apart his palm still held her.

'A contract sealed with a kiss.' His voice was not quite steady. 'More binding than ink.' He touched her lips lightly with his fingers. 'I'll write with details of travel arrangements and I'll see you in a fortnight.' Then he was gone, leaving Joanne staring at the closed door, her hand pressed to her still-burning lips.

CHAPTER FOUR

JOANNE looked resignedly across the desk at the pregnant lady in front of her. Mrs Dawson was huge. She was five months pregnant, but there was no way you could pick it by looking at her. Her rolls of fat concealed the pregnancy more effectively than could any designer maternity clothes.

'Mrs Dawson, you must have been eating more than your diet sheet permits. You've put on four kilos in a month—that's not all baby!'

'Beats me, Doc, and that's the truth.' The woman sat back in her chair and crossed her arms complacently. 'Must be fluid, I reckon. I don't eat no more than a sparrow.'

Some sparrow, Joanne thought with grim humour. If she kept putting on weight at her present rate she was heading for trouble.

'Mrs Dawson, if we can't stop your weight gain you run a serious risk of having to have this baby early. Already your blood-pressure is much higher than it should be.'

'Always has been high,' the lady replied with good humour. 'It's genetic.'

'You mean your parents have high blood-pressure?'

Mrs Dawson nodded cheerfully. 'Well, me dad still has. Me mum died of it.'

'And they were big people too?'

'Me mum was bigger 'n me. I'm one of the smaller

34

ones in the family. At least,' she eyed her bulging midriff doubtfully, 'I was before I got pregnant.'

Joanne shook her head slowly. She knew the advice she was giving was going to be ignored. Nevertheless she gave it, with as good a humour as possible.

'I want you to see the dietician before you go,' she said as Mrs Dawson rose to leave. Perhaps Pauline could succeed where she was so obviously failing. There was small chance of that, though. Mrs Dawson's history of obesity must date back from being overfed as a baby. At thirty there was little hope of repairing the damage. Their only hope was that they could teach her to care for the new baby more sensibly than she herself had been cared for.

She saw Mrs Dawson to the door with a small sigh of relief. The morning's work was over. She was trying to fit too much into these two short weeks. There were only four more days to go before she had to be on the plane to Strathleath Island. As Mrs Dawson's formidable bulk retreated from the doorway Barbara's much more compact figure appeared.

'Not another pregnant woman!' Joanne groaned. Theatrically. 'You're my nineteenth for this morning.'

'I'm only a little bit pregnant, though,' Barbara laughed. She gestured to the now empty corridor behind her. 'If I'm thirty-seven weeks, she must be at least fifty.'

Joanne grinned. 'I wouldn't be so smug if I were you. Have you looked at yourself from behind? Ouch!' She ducked as a magazine flew across the room at her. 'Enough. What can I do for you?'

'I came to pick you up.'

'Pick me up?' Joanne eyed her friend suspiciously. 'To go where?'

'Shopping,' Barbara responded gleefully. 'My very favourite pastime. Even more favourite when it's your money, not mine.'

Joanne frowned. 'Barbara, I'm down for another clinic this afternoon. I haven't got time for shopping.'

'Yes, you have.'

Joanne leaned back against the wall and eyed her friend dubiously. 'OK, Barbara, what have you done?'

'Well,' Barbara's eyes gleamed with mischief, 'I did just happen to run into Dr Carter and I did just happen to mention what a shame it was that you were going to have to rush off to Strathleath Island the day after you finished up here, with no time to pack or shop or anything.'

'And?' Joanne knew her boss. She wasn't due to finish until Friday, and she couldn't see Dr Carter considering shopping a good reason to finish early.

Barbara screwed up her nose. 'Well, I did just say how concerned Wayne was about you. And,' she added virtuously, 'I took the opportunity to ask how his wife was recovering from her gallstone operation.'

'Barbara! You incorrigible. . .' Joanne stared at her friend with a mixture of horror and admiration. 'Wayne would kill you if he knew.' Wayne had operated on Mrs Carter the week before and Joanne knew he wouldn't have charged his friend's wife for the operation. Dr Carter would have been in a poor position to resist pressure from Wayne's wife.

Barbara giggled. 'I know—most unprofessional. But desperate straits demand desperate measures, and I'm not going to allow my very best friend to leave for Strathleath Island looking like something the cat dragged in.'

'Barbara!'

'It's true.' Barbara was unrepentant. 'Anyway, Dr Carter, in his magnanimity, has given you today and tomorrow afternoon off. Apparently one of the rotating residents can fill in for you. Now,' she assumed a severe aspect, 'we have work to do. Get rid of your white coat, grab your bag and come.'

'Yes, ma'am.'

It was a strange experience, shopping for clothes with the knowledge that there was money enough and to spare for all the lovely creations Barbara kept producing. Barbara had always dressed with style and flair. As she led Joanne from one exclusive boutique to another the assistants greeted her as an old friend. While Joanne stood back, bemused, she and the various assistants rummaged through racks of garments, emerging to hold one after another in front of the hapless Joanne.

'Barbara, this is crazy,' Joanne expostulated. She looked doubtfully at her reflection, clad in a striking two-piece creation, a soft cream shirt slashed with crimson edging and a divided skirt cut almost indecently short. A crimson sash emphasised her tiny waist. 'This isn't me.'

'Of course it is,' Barbara said briskly. 'It was made for someone with your figure. Oh, for heaven's sake!' She wheeled to stare disgustedly at her own matronly figure. 'Take it off and pay for it before I turn green with envy.'

Joanne smiled perfunctorily and started stripping again. 'Barbara, be serious. It's all very well me buying these wonderful clothes, but I can't really wear them.'

'Why ever not?'

'Well. . .' Joanne paused and looked seriously at her

reflection. 'Barbara, they're all wrong. They may be gorgeous clothes, but they just look. . .well. . .'

'Wrong,' Barbara supplied helpfully.

'Yes,' Joanne said defiantly. 'I might be thin enough to wear them, but they're not meant for me.'

Barbara smiled and unexpectedly nodded in agreement. 'I know what you mean. I've been wondering how to broach it without hurting your feelings.'

Joanne choked on a bubble of laughter. 'Barbara, I do not believe you. Something the cat dragged in, I think I remember you calling me. Now if that's being sensitive to my feelings I'd hate to hear you deliberately set out to insult someone!'

Barbara grinned. 'Oh, well, just accept that it's all for your own good. You're right, of course. The problem is your hair. It's still in a time-lock, somewhere about my grandmother's generation. Come on, pay for these. We've got an appointment.'

It was too much for Joanne. Helplessly she let the tide pick her up and carry her where it willed. 'Where?'

'Jean-Jacques.'

Barbara's hairdresser was a studious little man in his late fifties. He eyed Joanne's hair with distaste over the top of his spectacles.

'What a thing to do with a head of hair.' He pulled the pins from the harsh knot, letting the fine blonde hair cascade down to Joanne's waist. 'Ah.' It was a purr of satisfaction. His hand lifted the hair and ran through it. 'Never, never do such a dreadful thing to this hair again.' He held it up, feeling the effect of the hair's natural wave while he watched the reflection of Joanne's face.

'I don't think I want it short,' Joanne broke in in

panic as he produced his scissors. 'It's always been long.'

'You think I would take all this lovely hair off?' he demanded, shocked.

Joanne resigned herself. The result, she had to acknowledge an hour later, was amazing.

The sheer bulk of hair had gone. Joanne had always thought of her hair as straight, but clever layering had released the weight, allowing the natural wave back into the hair. It bounced and shone, tiny tendrils wisping around her ears and falling in waves on to her shoulders. Her face broadened under the soft waves, taking away the harsh, strained look Joanne had always associated with herself.

'I'll never be able to tie it back,' she said dubiously. 'It's all different lengths.'

'Exactly,' Monsieur Jacques said in satisfaction. 'You leave it as it is, as it was meant to be. Your hair, Dr Tynon, is beautiful.'

'It's not just the hair,' Barbara retorted, heaving herself to her feet from the chair where she had been supervising operations. 'Dr Tynon is beautiful.'

Monsieur Jacques stood back and looked critically at his fair client. Finally he nodded. 'I stand corrected,' he responded to Barbara. 'Dr Tynon is indeed beautiful.'

There was one more stop.

'For heaven's sake, you must be exhausted,' Joanne told Barbara as they left the hair salon. 'I am, and I'm not eight months pregnant. Can't we stop now?'

'No fear,' Barbara responded emphatically. 'I'm having the time of my life. Honestly, Joanne, you can't imagine how much I've wanted to do this over the

years. Now I've got the opportunity don't you dare
deprive me of it!'

'But there's nothing left to buy!' Joanne's voice was
almost a wail. 'Dresses, shorts, blouses, swimsuits,
shoes, trousers. . . For heaven's sake, we've bought
more than enough for two of me.'

'Undies.'

'I beg your pardon?'

'You heard me.' Barbara grinned and motioned
towards a tiny shop. 'Undies.'

'Barbara!' Barbara had reached the entrance and
beckoned Joanne inside. 'There's nothing wrong with
my underwear,' she said in a savage whisper.

'If you happen to be a Girl Scout,' Barbara agreed
sagely. 'Or my great-aunt Mildred. But you're not. Oh,
look!'

Joanne looked. There on a mannequin was the most
perfect piece of frivolity she had ever seen. It was a
robe of pure Swiss cotton, exquisitely smocked with
white thread on a white background. The only colour
was a scattering of tiny French knots, worked in the
palest of blue. Under the robe was a nightgown. The
thinnest of satin straps held the pure white gown from
slipping over the mannequin's breasts. The rest of the
gown floated down to ankle length. The sheerness of
the Swiss cotton clung to and revealed every curve of
the mannequin. Only where the open robe fell against
the soft nightdress could it be called the least
respectable.

'Oh,' sighed Barbara softly, 'isn't that the most
gorgeous thing you've ever seen?'

'You'd never buy it?' Joanne grinned. Then at the
look on Barbara's face she laughed incredulously.

'Barbara, you're a respectable married woman. What on earth would Wayne say?'

'I know exactly what Wayne would say.' She tore her eyes reluctantly from the model. 'But as you're not a respectable married lady I'm certainly not going to tell you, and I'm shocked that you could even ask. Now, back to work. Into the fitting-room with you.'

Joanne emerged with her nice sensible knickers and bras replaced by ones she just knew good girls shouldn't own. Her protests simply produced giggles from Barbara, and finally she resigned herself to the lacy items produced by an entranced assistant.

As she approached the counter, bearing rather self-consciously a handful of scanty garments, the sales assistant was putting the final wrapping on a large box.

'What on earth is that?' Joanne asked suspiciously. None of the wispy little pieces she was buying warranted such packaging.

Barbara grinned and handed her the box. 'This, Joanne, is my farewell gift to you. I may have deprived you of your Girl Scout knickers, but you can still follow the Scout motto: "Be prepared"! And have fun.'

Joanne whirled to look at the mannequin, last seen robed in stunning white. Her suspicions were confirmed. The mannequin was bare. The transformation of Joanne Tynon was complete.

CHAPTER FIVE

JOANNE sat on the upper deck of the *Sea Mist* trying unsuccessfully to control the excitement welling within her.

On landing at Cairns she had been met with apologies from the airport staff. Owing to a mechanical problem there would be no plane across to Strathleath until the morning. Would Joanne like accommodation arranged or would she like to take the ferry?

For Joanne the choice was obvious. She sat now watching the bow of the boat cut a white swathe through the sunlit water. The sun warmed her hungrily upturned face and stirred the soft waves of shining hair. She was free. The bleakness of Melbourne's winter and her dreary past was behind her. Ahead. . . Well, she had no idea what lay ahead. The prospect was delicious.

She was momentarily distracted by a heated altercation at the rear of the boat, and shaded her eyes to see what was happening. One of the last passengers to board the boat had been a woman of about Joanne's age—but there, Joanne thought, the resemblance ended. Everything about her proclaimed wealth and indulgence, from the sophisticated cut of her gleaming black hair to her immaculate matched leather luggage. Joanne was happy with her new wardrobe, but this girl's appearance made her feel a country bumpkin.

The difference between the two girls wasn't just in appearance. Where Joanne was eagerly soaking in every aspect of this trip, the lady creating the disturbance at the rear of the boat was in no mood to appreciate the scenery. She had boarded the boat late, bemoaning the airline's ineptitude which had forced her to take such an obviously undesirable means of getting to Strathleath. Now she had discovered there were no seats to be had under the shaded canopy of the upper deck, she was faced with either sitting in the sun or descending to sit in the stuffy lounge below deck. Finally, after directing a tirade against the unmoving passengers, the woman went below. Those on the upper deck heaved a communal sigh of relief. Joanne felt a twinge of sympathy for the boat staff, trying to placate such a difficult passenger, but forgot her immediately she turned back to face the breeze. Thank heaven it wasn't her problem.

Strathleath loomed ahead of them, and Joanne eagerly took in every detail. From this distance it seemed almost uninhabited, a mountainous mass of land surging upward from the sea bed.

Gradually the ferry drew closer and Joanne could make out buildings, a town nestled in a cove forming a natural harbour. They were heading for a jetty with an access road blasted from the cliff face on one side of the cove.

The water here was shallow, the deep blue of the sea lightening to a blue-green. As the boat edged closer to the jetty Joanne looked over the side and was caught, mesmerised by the myriad forms of life below the surface. Fish of every size and colour could be seen darting under and around the boat. When Joanne finally looked up the ferry's ropes were being fastened to the jetty and Cam was standing directly above her.

He was searching through the mill of passengers. His

gaze flicked her briefly and went on. Joanne was aware of a surge of pleasure at the sight of him. He was wearing casual drill trousers with an open-necked shirt and his dark hair was tousled in the sea breeze. Joanne looked up at the deep, seeking eyes and felt a tremor of anticipation. Those eyes were looking for her.

She picked up her bag and made her way to the gangplank, towards the searching figure. As she reached the solid jetty she paused, her eyes widening in shock. Attached possessively to Cam Maddon's hand was a small boy of about five years of age. He wore a pair of grubby shorts, an equally disreputable T-shirt and, on his left leg, a metal caliper. There was no mistaking his parentage. His dark eyes moved in unison with his father's, searching, frowning, trying to identify the person his father had brought him to meet.

Joanne took a deep breath and moved forward, her hand outstretched. 'Cam—here I am. Thank you for coming to meet me.'

Cam swung round. His eyes met hers and stared incredulously. His gaze dropped and raked her from her elegant sandals to her soft curls.

'What the hell have you done to yourself?' His voice was an explosion of disbelief.

Joanne's hand dropped and her smile faded. 'Pardon?'

'You heard what I said. What the hell have you done to yourself?'

Around them people were pausing to gaze curiously at the participants in this odd interchange. Joanne was aware of the little boy, looking up at her with wide, astonished eyes. She struggled to contain her rising anger and attempted a smile.

'My new image doesn't meet with yur approval?'

The pale green frock with full circle skirt and matching short-sleeved jacket had been her choice rather than Barbara's and was one of the more demure items in her radically revised wardrobe.

'It certainly does not!' Cam's voice was like a blast of ice water, dousing the warmth of Joanne's delicious excitement. 'I want an assistant. If I'd wanted a fashion plate I would have advertised for one.'

Joanne carefully put down the holdall she was carrying and met his gaze with outward calm. Inwardly she was coming steadily and surely to the boil, but on the surface she was still under control. The hum around them had dropped away. She was miserably aware that most of the people on the jetty would know who Cam was and perhaps why she was here. Perhaps some of them could end up being her patients. Her tone, when she finally spoke, matched his for iciness.

'Mr Maddon, I am sorry if my appearance does not meet your apparently stringent requirements. This, however, seems neither the time nor the place to discuss it. If you have indeed come to collect me, perhaps you would be good enough to assist me in locating my suitcases.' She gestured to the array of luggage being unloaded. 'If you wish, you can continue your criticism later. In private!'

She ended up hissing the last two words at him through gritted teeth, but, even though they had been uttered quietly, it seemed the conversation had been overheard by nearly every person on the jetty. Cheers and good-natured applause broke out from the crowd. Joanne was aware that many of the glances at her flushed countenance were admiring, but she was too angry to dredge up a grin. How dared this man humiliate her so publicly?

Cam's countenance was thunderous. Pushing through the crush of people, he took the two suitcases offered by a bemused boatman and headed off towards the parking bay at the end of the jetty. The small boy stamped off after him and, with a helpless shrug of her shoulders, Joanne followed.

'Cam! Darling!'

Cam stopped as if he had been shot. For a long moment his figure stood immobile, with Joanne and the little boy brought up short behind him. Then he wheeled around. His face was rigid with shock.

'Lindy!'

Joanne's mind clicked back to the conversation she had had with Barbara two weeks before. 'He finally married one. . . Lindy was an actress.' It fitted. The woman coming towards them, her hands outstretched in greeting, would have to be a model or an actress. No one else could wear such magnificent clothes with the assurance and grace she did. Joanne looked down at the confused little boy standing beside her. There was a resemblance. Here, then, was his mother.

'Cam! What amazing good luck to find you here. I was going to surprise you!'

'What the hell are you doing here?'

As greetings go, it could have been better, Joanne decided, but Lindy's smile didn't falter.

'I came to see you, of course. And our son.' Her clear tones could be heard along the length of the jetty. By now they had quite an audience. 'My goodness.' This was a long-drawn-out exclamation as Lindy looked down at the small boy. She stooped to take two small hands. 'Hello, there. Do you remember me?'

The child pulled back urgently and broke her clasp,

retreating behind his father's legs. From there he glared at the modish vision before them.

Cam reached down and swung the little boy up into his arms. 'Of course he doesn't, Lindy. He was only six months old when you left.'

'You've never even shown him a photo?' The girl's voice was shocked.

'Lindy,' Cam's voice sounded weary and defeated, 'the only photographs of you show you as a blonde. Tom thinks his mother has lovely curling golden hair. You do a chameleon act, you take the consequences.' His glance swept from Lindy back to Joanne, and Joanne flushed and cringed under his enveloping scorn. 'Come on.' He addressed Joanne and started walking again towards the car.

'But. . . I haven't got my luggage. . .' Lindy's voice was a cry behind them. Cam stopped again and turned to face her.

'Lindy, what you do is your business. I have no idea what you're here for, or where you're staying and I am not interested. If you wish to see Tom while you're here I suggest you ring at some stage during your time on the island and arrange it. You'll find me at the hospital.' His words were clipped, his face set and hard. 'Meanwhile, I have work to do.' He stood back to let Joanne precede him, then turned his back on his audience.

They entered the car in silence. It was large and comfortable, but Joanne was in no mood to relax. Her lovely bubble had burst. The scene on the jetty was the stuff that nightmares were made of. For the first time she acknowledged to herself that she was undeniably attracted to Cam Maddon. Those few moments on the jetty where he had shown how much he disliked her transformation, and then her discovery of the presence of his beautiful wife, had destroyed the tiny flame of unacknowledged hope inside her. Cam stared straight ahead as the car pulled up the steep incline to the town. Heaven knew what he was thinking. The silence was finally broken by a small voice from the back seat.

'Who was that lady on the jetty?'

'Tom, I'll tell you when we get home, OK?'

'Well, who's this lady?' He turned to stare at Joanne. His tone was of one who considered he had been ill-used. 'I don't even know your name.'

'It's Joanne.' Joanne swivelled in her seat and gave the little boy a quick smile. His father might be an arrogant toad, but she didn't see why she should punish him for his father's sins.

'The lady's name is Dr Tynon.' Cam's voice was curt. 'You know that.'

'Yes, but I wanted to know her real name,' the child explained. 'Mine's Tom—Thomas really, but no one calls me that except when I'm in trouble. Can I call you Joanne?'

'Of course.'

'Tom!' Cam's voice carried a warning.

'Dad, it's OK. She won't mind.' Tom's voice was patient, as if explaining something to someone who was not very bright. 'Joanne's nice. And,' he continued, his voice growing defiant as if contradicting something he had been told earlier, 'she's pretty.'

Joanne looked across at Cam's set mouth and stern eyes, and then around at the endearing face in the back seat, and her anger dissolved. Cam was clearly under stress which she didn't understand. While she knew she was going to have to tread carefully with her new boss, at least this grubby little urchin could be a friend. She gave him a grin, cast another covert glance at the driver and spent the rest of the journey diligently admiring the scenery.

The hospital was a delight. Set behind the town, it nestled in a sprawling tropical garden. Massive flame trees sprayed splashes of crimson overhead. Below, the softer colours of hibiscus provided contrast to the lush greenery. The garden was filled with birds, their calls echoing through that lovely, quiet place.

The hospital itself was a long wooden building with wide verandas on all sides. Patients were settled on big wicker chairs on the veranda or down on the lawn under the shade of the huge trees. For those too ill to be outside the floor-length windows of each room were open to their full extent, allowing the soft breezes to flow through the wards.

As they drew to a halt in front of the hospital, Joanne had to resist an urge to pinch herself to make sure she wasn't dreaming. The contrast between this place and the huge metropolitan hospital where she had spent her working life was staggering.

Cam's introductions were perfunctory to say the least, but Joanne gained the impression of a nursing staff who were welcoming and interested in the new doctor. There was little time for pleasantries. Cam cut short any attempts at conversation by either Joanne or the nurses who came to meet her and ushered her swiftly through the hospital corridors to a tiny apartment at the rear. Her suitcases were placed inside the door. Tom gave her a quick apologetic grin and she was left alone.

It suited Joanne. Her mind was filled with a muddle of impressions. She was tired and confused, and badly needed time to herself. She investigated her new home and was pleased with what she found, a lovely light living-room with french windows leading out to the garden, a tiny bedroom dominated by a huge ceiling-fan and an immaculately clean kitchenette and bathroom. It was more than she needed. She flung all the windows wide to allow the lovely warm breezes to flow through the rooms and set to work unpacking.

With the unpacking finished Joanne was at a loss. The kitchenette had the wherewithal to make a cup of tea and a slice of toast, but it certainly wasn't equipped for meals. She had been offered a light meal on the plane some hours previously and was now aware of the need to eat. She looked at the sparse contents of the refrigerator in distaste. She didn't feel like celebrating her first night in her new job with tea and toast.

A knock at the door interrupted her hungry reflections. It was Cam.

'I expect you'd like to see around the hospital.' Whatever inner turmoil he was undergoing through the sudden reappearance of his wife had obviously been thrust aside to be dealt with in private. Here was Mr Maddon, surgeon, ready to show an out-of-favour employee her duties.

Joanne was having trouble reconciling this harsh-voiced man with the Cam Maddon who had kissed her farewell a fortnight before. Her brow creased in puzzlement and concern as she looked up at him.

'Yes, please, Cam, I would like to see the hospital.'

He stood back to let her precede him and they walked silently together towards the wards.

His monosyllabic conversation eased slightly as the tour of the building progressed. Joanne was eager to learn all she could about the little hospital and, ignoring her companion's lack of enthusiasm, asked question after question. Short of sacking her on the spot and sending her packing back to Melbourne, Cam could hardly refuse to answer her questions, and gradually his enthusiasm for the place and Joanne's interest came together to make them talk. It was clear that Cam had done much of the hard work in making the hospital the efficient unit it appeared. He talked of the building, the equipment and the staff with the pride of achievement.

Joanne was impressed. She had expected very few of the medical amenities she had enjoyed at her former hospital and had been expecting to have to send many patients to Cairns. With the equipment available at Strathleath it seemed only the patients requiring major surgery or specific specialist attention would need to make the trip.

Cam used his tour with Joanne to do his evening ward round. The patients greeted him with the affection of a trusted friend, and Joanne started to see a hitherto unseen advantage of practising in a small community. It would be pleasant to know her patients' backgrounds.

He introduced her again to the hospital matron. Matron Wheeler was a pleasant-faced woman in her fifties who provided the first real welcome Joanne had received.

'We're really glad to have you here, Dr Tynon. If there's anything you need you have only to tell us. If you're not happy here it won't be the fault of the nursing staff.' She cast a worried glance up at Cam before disappearing to answer a bell. Her reaction left

Joanne wondering how Cam had treated other assistants.

She reappeared in a moment, her worried look deepening. 'I'm sorry to interrupt your tour, Mr Maddon, but could you come down to Casualty? Little Chris Tanner's just been brought in by his mum and dad. He doesn't look too bright.'

'Certainly, Matron.' Cam turned and strode down the corridor, assuming Joanne would follow.

It didn't need a detailed examination to reveal that the seven-year-old they found in the examination cubicle was very ill. He was ashen-faced and quiet, with the limpness seen only in severely ill children. Joanne stood at the rear of the cubicle and watched while Cam gently examined him. His hands explored the little boy's abdomen, and the child winced with pain as Cam pressed down on his right side, then gave a moan as the fingers released their pressure. Joanne grimaced. Rebound tenderness—appendicitis with probable peritonitis.

'Have you ever heard of appendicitis?' Cam was speaking softly to the little boy.

The child's head nodded almost imperceptibly, his eyes clouded with pain. 'My brother's had it. He had his appendix out.' The voice was a thread.

'Well, you know all about it.' The harsh-faced man who had greeted Joanne had disappeared. In his place was a surgeon whose only concern was to reassure a frightened child. He smiled gently into the terrified eyes. 'It's your appendix that's hurting you so much. What about Dr Tynon and me,' he gestured behind him and moved aside so Chris could see Joanne, 'giving you something to let you go to sleep, and then taking it out, just like the doctors did for your brother? Good idea?'

'Yes, please.' The voice was shaky but decisive and the fear fading from his eyes.

'Good decision, Chris.' Cam's voice suggested it had been the child's choice all along. 'Now, I need your mum and dad to sign a couple of forms for me, and while they're doing that Matron will stay with you. They'll be back with you before you go to sleep, though. OK?' At the slight nod of assent he ushered the worried parents out.

Preparations were made swiftly. If indeed the appendix had burst, the sooner they operated the better. As Joanne scrubbed she thought how much more at risk the little boy would have been if she had not arrived tonight. The last thing he needed now was a time-consuming journey to Cairns, but with only one doctor available there would have been no choice.

The operation was difficult. The appendix had burst, leaving a mess which had to be scrupulously cleared to avoid infection. By the time the drainage tube had been inserted and the wound closed Joanne had reinforced her previous impression of Cam Maddon. This man had skills which would be almost wasted on such a small population. It would be a pleasure to work for him, providing she could somehow change his attitude towards her.

The anaesthetic took all her attention, but finally Cam completed his task, the anaesthetic was reversed and the child's natural rhythmic breathing resumed. Joanne gave a sigh of relief. No matter how many anaesthetics she did she felt she would never get over the strain of the patient's life being completely in her hands. She glanced briefly, from her position at the child's head, at Cam's intent face. It showed strain not explained by the pressures of the operation. What sort of stress was he enduring, she wondered, bringing up a small boy on his own, with a wife who wanted no part of him? Or did she? What did Lindy's appearance on the island signify?

As Chris was wheeled back to the ward they cleaned up in silence. Joanne concentrated on neatly folding the surgical gown before placing it carefully in the bin destined for the laundry. This was going to be impossible. How could she work in such a hostile environment?

'He'll be OK.' Cam's brusque tones broke the silence and Joanne almost jumped. 'I'm pretty sure it's clear.'

'He's a bit young to be coping with a peritoneal abscess,' Joanne said softly.

'Well, with any luck it won't come to that. I'll hit him hard with antibiotic through the drip. It would have been a lot worse if you hadn't been here and I'd had to send him to Cairns. Do you want to come with me while I talk to his parents?'

It wasn't an apology, but it was definitely a peace-offering, Joanne thought. The blatant hostility had lessened. She, however, wasn't prepared to forgive and forget quite so easily. Did he expect her to be grateful just because he wasn't insulting her?

'No, thanks.' In fact, there was a more pressing need for Joanne than accompanying Cam. Her stomach was sending her very firm messages. Even tea and toast in her flat was looking good.

'Suit yourself.' He turned abruptly and departed.

Joanne made her way slowly back to her flat, stopping to exchange pleasantries for a few moments with Matron Wheeler. She thought briefly of investigating the hospital kitchen, but decided against it. Hospital dinner would be long over. As she swung open the door to her flat she was assailed by the smell of food. Casserole, she thought joyfully. The smell was definitely coming from her kitchenette. She walked through the living-room to the dividing door and stopped in surprise. Seated at her table was Cam's small son.

'Hello.' His tone was grave, eerily reminiscent of his father's.

'Hello.'

'I thought you might be hungry.' He gestured backward towards the stove. 'Your dinner's in there.'

Joanne felt an absurd desire to laugh at this serious, pyjama-clad child, sitting with his feet not quite reaching the floor. She suppressed the urge sternly and met his look.

'Thank you, Tom. How did you guess I'd be hungry?'

'I knew you would be.' He sighed importantly. 'Dad and me made a casserole this afternoon to share with you tonight. He put it in the oven before we went to the boat. Then was cross and that other lady came. When we got home he said the other lady is my mother and he had to go and see her and Mrs Robb would give me tea in the hospital kitchen and put me to bed like she nearly always does. And she did.' The voice rose in indignation. 'Early! Only, then I remembered our casserole was still in the oven and you'd be all by yourself, so I brought it over to you. You were out, but I knew you'd come back if I waited long enough.'

'Oh, Tom!'

'It's OK,' he replied placatingly. 'I knew Dad would worry about me burning myself, so I was very careful and wore oven mitts and everything, and I sneaked across the lawn so Mrs Robb wouldn't see me and send me back to bed. Are you pleased?'

Joanne reached out and ruffled a small head. 'Tom, I'm lost for words.'

'Does that mean you're pleased?'

Joanne grinned. 'Pleased beyond words. However, I have a small worry in the back of my mind that your dad may not be all that happy.'

'You may be right.' The voice came from the open door leading on to the veranda and they both started guiltily. Cam Maddon walked in and stood gazing sternly at his son. 'What on earth do you think you're doing?'

'Joanne was hungry.' Tom's voice was belligerent. 'You said yourself we had to make something for her dinner.'

'I'm sure Dr Tynon is more than capable of making her own dinner.'

'There's nothing here for her to eat. You said there wouldn't be, and it would be kinder to have her for dinner when she's only just arrived. And then you forgot.'

The eyes of father and son met, each glaring at the other. Joanne's lips twitched. Two iron wills meeting. She turned her back on them, reached down and retrieved the casserole from the oven before turning back.

'Tom, it really was a lovely thought, but it was unnecessary. What your father says is true. There's plenty here for me to eat. This is obviously for your father's tea, and I'd hate to deprive him of it.' She flashed Cam her sweetest smile, put the casserole on the table in front of him, then walked around to the screen door and held it open, waiting for them to go.

Tom's face fell ludicrously and his eyes filled with tears. He was only a very little boy, Joanne thought with sympathy, but there wasn't much she could do to alleviate the situation.

'Why can't you share it?' His voice hiccupped on a sob.

'I think,' Cam said resignedly, his eyes on Joanne's face, 'that perhaps that would be a good idea. You're right, Tom. It was meant to be shared, after all. But you, my boy, need to be in bed. If Dr Tynon agrees——'

'Joanne!' Tom broke in mutinously.

'I stand corrected. If Joanne agrees, perhaps we could all adjourn to our flat. Then we could polish off one rather overcooked casserole while you go to sleep.'

'I'm not sleepy.'

His father just grinned, reached down and swung him up into his arms. 'If I carry this one, Dr Tynon——'

'Joanne!' Tom repeated.

'OK, OK. If I carry Tom, Joanne, do you think you can carry the casserole?'

There was no choice. Tom was regarding Joanne in triumph. She spread her hands helplessly. 'Are you sure?'

'Of course we're sure,' Tom said firmly. 'Aren't we, Dad?'

Cam dredged up a grin. 'Yes, Joanne, we appear to be sure.'

It was a strange meal. Cam's flat was very like Joanne's, only marginally larger. With the casserole once again in the oven, Joanne was left to her own devices in the living-room while Cam put Tom to bed. It was a sparse place for a child to be brought up, Joanne thought. The place was furnished for functionality rather than comfort, and it was scrupulously clean. The faint smell of hospital disinfectant told her that hospital cleaners were responsible for Cam's housekeeping. Nothing was out of place. There was little to suggest that this was a child's home.

Outside on the veranda there was a table and chairs. Repelled by the clinical cleanliness of the flat, Joanne searched in the kitchenette for cutlery and crockery and set the table outside for dinner. She was assuming Cam hadn't eaten. Perhaps he'd had dinner with Lindy. Either way, he was going to eat again. She was darned if she'd sit here and eat alone under his critical eyes.

The subdued murmur of voices from the bedroom ceased. Joanne stayed seated where she was until Cam appeared bearing two laden plates. He set them down and disappeared again, only to reappear bearing a bottle of wine and two glasses.

'There's no need. . .' Joanne expostulated, embarrassed.

'According to my son, there's every need,' Cam replied with a wry smile. 'I've just been given a thorough dressing-down.'

Joanne smiled. 'He's a sweetheart.'

'He's a good kid,' Cam agreed, filling her glass. 'A trifle confused at the moment, but he'll cope.'

'I gather he hasn't seen much of his mother.' Joanne's words hung between them, strung out on the quiet of the balmy night. Joanne bit her lip, but the words had been said, and there was no way she could retract them. Finally Cam finished eating, pushed his plate back and rose.

'Look, I'm sorry you had to be part of that scene at

the jetty. I had no way of knowing Lindy was going to be on that boat, it shook me.'

'I understand that,' Joanne said gently. 'I seem to recall, though, that there was a scene before you even saw Lindy.'

'With you, you mean?'

'With me.' Joanne swallowed, but the words had to be said if she was to achieve a working relationship with this man. 'I don't enjoy being told off in public, and I still don't understand what I've done to deserve such public censure.'

'Don't you?'

'No.'

'Not even after you've seen Lindy?'

Joanne's eyes opened wide with surprise. 'What on earth has your wife to do with me?'

'My ex-wife.' He spat the words.

'Very well—your ex-wife.' Joanne stood up and pushed her chair in. The sound of the cane against the bare boards reverberated between them. Cam stood back against the veranda rails, a dark, enigmatic shadow. 'Why should your problems with your ex-wife mean that your assistant should be forbidden to buy a new dress?'

'A new dress? A new self, more like. The conscientious, hard-working woman I met in Melbourne isn't you.'

'Did my new dress and new hairstyle prevent me from giving Chris Tanner a competent anaesthetic?' she demanded.

'That's got nothing to do with it.'

'Like hell it hasn't!' she exploded. 'It's got everything to do with it. If you don't like my work you can criticise me, Cam Maddon. Nothing else is any of your business.'

'The image you present to patients is my business.' Cam's voice was hard and gravelly.

'Then you'd better sack me now, because this is me. I don't intend to go back to being a dowd because you say so.'

'What the hell do you think you're playing at?' He left the veranda rail and came towards her. Instinctively Joanne moved backwards, towards the step. 'You're just the same as Lindy. You think you just have to step into elegant clothes and throw on some French perfume and the poor sod will fall all over again.'

Joanne gasped. 'Of all the arrogant. . .! What makes you think I want anything to do with you, Cam Maddon?'

'Don't you?' he goaded. 'Don't you?' He reached out and held her, his hands gripping her arms until she cried out. 'Isn't this what it's all about?' He stood immobile looking down at her stunned and frightened face. His mouth twisted into a bitter laugh before he brought it down hard on hers.

Shock held Joanne immobile. Cam's kiss was hard, merciless, as if exacting revenge from pain inflicted. Who was this cold, angry man who was pressing his mouth on hers? Somewhere in the recesses of her mind was the memory of another kiss, a soft, sweet discovery between two people who had responded to each other with pleasure. Where was the Cam who had cared for her and kissed her goodbye only two weeks before?

She stood passively, allowing him to hold her as he willed. His hands were under her arms, pulling her up to meet his face. She felt no response to the pressure of his mouth on hers.

Finally he let her go. She regained her feet and stood speechlessly before him. She found she was studying the V of his collar, where the dark hairs stood out against the white cloth. Her overwhelming sensation was numbness. She couldn't move. She didn't know whether she wanted to.

For a long moment he stayed looking down at the top of her head. Finally she raised her eyes and met his, her eyes reflecting hurt and bewilderment.

'Damn!'

His curse hung in the air between them. Out on a lawn some night bird started up a long, low chatter of sound.

The third kiss was better. Cam reached down and took Joanne's face between his hands. Mutely she turned her face upward, waiting. She felt about fourteen. I'm exposed to this man, she thought helplessly. I shouldn't be here. What am I doing?

She knew, though, as soon as his lips met hers again. Here was the Cam who she knew. This man did things to her that she hadn't thought were possible. She felt her body light and respond to his in a warmth of peace and certainty.

Her lips softly parted, welcoming the searching tongue, moving hers in return. His tongue ran against her small white teeth and back into the moist recesses of her mouth. She felt her own tongue respond, moving to accommodate his, investigating on her own.

It was right. This man was right for her. Joanne's body stirred in acknowledgement of her surety.

His hands began a gentle exploration. The flimsy cotton frock was no barrier. His hands ran down her sides, against her thighs. They stayed there, stroking gently until Joanne's body felt as if it were a pinnacle of fire. She pressed herself into him, exulting in the hard maleness of his body.

The fingers ceased their stroking and moved upward, in through the low neckline of her frock, slipping down the straps of her flimsy bra to cup the ripeness of each taut nipple. Still his tongue moved inside her mouth, demanding her total capitulation. Joanne was lost, swirling in a mist of pleasure, pain, she knew not what. Her body had never felt like this before. This man was all that mattered, this strength against her, these eyes that pierced her inmost being.

Then it was over. Suddenly the hands were hard again, but instead of holding they were thrusting her away, breaking the exquisite contact of body against body. Joanne staggered and would have fallen. The hands steadied her and withdrew.

'You see?' Cam's voice was hoarse and ragged. 'I'm right—you're just like her.'

Joanne took a sobbing breath and looked up at the man in front of her. What was happening? Had this been some type of stupid test? A test which she'd failed? For a long moment there was silence, then Joanne reached out and struck as hard as she could. The ring of hand against cheek resounded through the night. Joanne turned and fled across the lawn to the sanctuary of her own apartment.

CHAPTER SIX

JOANNE woke from a troubled sleep, dreaming that someone was calling her name. For a moment she was confused. She lay back on the soft pillows, trying to adjust to being in this sun-drenched room rather than her Melbourne home. It was warm already.

She sat up, pulling the sheet around her. The memories of the night before flooded back, and she cringed in remembrance. She had gone to sleep vowing to get on the first flight out of Strathleath. So much for her brave new life!

'Joanne!' It hadn't been part of the dream. There was a scratching on the door, and it came again, a child's demanding call. 'Joanne!'

'Come in,' she called. Ten seconds later Tom's small form was seated solidly on her lap.

'I knew you'd be awake. Dad told me I was not to bother you, but I knew you'd want to see me. You do, don't you?' He peered anxiously up at her.

Joanne grinned. Her problems receded in the face of this urchin's charm. 'Of course I do. I've been lonely ever since I woke up.'

'Really?'

'Scout's honour.'

'Well,' he said on a note of satisfaction, 'it's just as well I came.'

'Is your dad up?' Joanne asked, then mentally chastised herself for her interest.

'Of course.' Tom's voice was scornful. 'He gets up almost as early as me. He's doing his rounds.'

'Tell me,' Joanne's forehead creased in puzzlement, 'who looks after you when your dad is working?'

'They all do,' Tom said in a voice of one explaining the obvious.

'All?'

'The people at the hospital,' he said patiently. 'They're all my friends. Is my leg hurting you?' He swung the calipered leg off her lap and deposited it on the bedclothes so she wasn't bearing its weight.

'It's fine,' Joanne assured him. 'It's not too heavy.'

'Do you want to know what's wrong with it?'

'If you want to tell me.'

'OK.' He wriggled in to make himself more comfortable and then proceeded on an obviously well-rehearsed story. 'It's talipes equinovarus.'

Joanne nodded. 'You know, I thought it might be that.'

'Really?' he demanded suspiciously. 'Nobody ever knows what it is.'

'Well, I am a doctor,' Joanne said apologetically.

'What does it mean, then?' he asked.

'Are you testing my medical knowledge?' Joanne grinned. 'OK then, Tom Maddon, talipes equinovarus means you've got a downward-inverted ankle. It's not quite at the right angle to allow you to run and jump like most children. By the look of it, though, I'd say yours is not too bad a case. If you keep wearing your caliper I'd say by the time you're as big as me you'll hardly have a problem, and will be able to throw your caliper away forever.'

'Really?' His face was still creased in suspicion.

'Really.'

'That's just what my dad says,' he said cheerfully, swung his legs down and slid off the bed.

'Where are you off to now?'

'Dad told me Chris Tanner had his appendix out last night. Dad says he's doing really well and I can pop my head around the door and say good morning, only I'm not to go in. Dad says he needs rest.' With the virtuous air of a ministering angel off to do his rounds, Tom departed.

Joanne rose slowly and crossed to the window. The early morning sun was glinting on the last of the dew on the lawn. Above, in the trees, flocks of brightly coloured birds called to each other as they swooped up and resettled. Anywhere else their brilliant plumage would make them stand out. The colours of the tropical garden camouflaged them perfectly, however, and Joanne could only pick them out by following the sound and the movement. Beyond the trees there was a tantalising glimpse of sun on water, the glitter of the sea.

It looked close. Perhaps there was a bay below the garden. Joanne glanced at her bedside clock. Seven o'clock. She wouldn't be expected to front for duty until nine on her first morning, and if today was likely to be her only day on the island perhaps she could explore. Swiftly she donned her swimsuit, pulled a soft sarong over the top and made her way towards the sea.

A path starting at the edge of the garden meandered through the trees and undergrowth. It was wide and clearly marked, obviously a well-used track. After her rush to escape the hospital Joanne slowed down, taking time to enjoy the smell of the bush and the cries of the birds.

The path ended abruptly, leaving her standing at the

edge of a tiny inlet. Golden sand, already warm, oozed into her sandals. Tiny waves lapped the shore, and the water beckoned with turquoise brilliance. In seconds Joanne's sarong and sandals were forgotten, a crumpled heap high on the sand.

For a glorious half-hour the oppression of her welcome the day before, the humiliation of Cam's embraces, were forgotten. She swam strongly back and forth across the bay, the sheer physical effort calming her. As she reached the smooth rocks on either side of the little inlet she dived and turned, sending schools of little fish darting in panic. Finally, tired but at peace with herself, she rolled over and floated lazily on her back. Cam Maddon was an arrogant, chauvinistic male with a wife and son. There was no future in the physical attraction he felt for him. Look where it had got her last night. Remembrance flooded back and she fought to retain her calm.

So? Could she stay working here? Yes, her body screamed at her, soaking in the bliss of the sea and the sun on her face. No, said her head. There is nothing to be gained by a partnership with Cam Maddon except conflict.

While her mind had been busy, Joanne had been floating gradually towards the rocks. As she reached them she pulled herself up on to a flat, rocky ledge and sat looking back to the beach. To her horror she saw a familiar male figure emerge from the dark tunnel of the path. Cam. She pulled herself backwards in dismay. She was not ready for confrontation here, like this. When next she saw him she wanted to be in her white coat, stethoscope around her neck, a fellow professional.

Cam saw the pile of clothes tossed carelessly almost

at his feet. He stood, shading his eyes from the glare, trying to make out the location of their owner. Finally his gaze settled on the distant figure of Joanne, perched on her ledge. Without taking his eyes off her he stripped to the bathing-trunks he was wearing underneath his clothes and dived into the clear water.

Joanne was caught in awful indecision. Should she abandon her ledge and swim back to shore? There was no way she could outswim him. His smoothly muscled body was coursing through the water at three times or more her best speed. Finally she simply sat and waited until the dark head emerged from the water under her rock. He swung himself easily out of the water and stood, his wet body glistening in the sun.

For a moment Joanne sat, allowing the streams of water from his wet body to fall on her. Then she stood up, shakily. Her attempt to meet him face to face was a dismal failure; her eyes were somewhere below his chin.

'This is my rock.' She sounded like a petulant six-year-old, she realised, and would have bitten the words back. He grinned.

'So push me off.'

She glared at him and dived neatly into the water, setting off with determination towards the shore. It was only a few strokes before she realised she was being matched, stroke for stroke. She swam on grimly, unable to ignore the powerful presence beside her. Finally she reached the shallows, found her feet and started wading towards the beach. As she reached the low line of breakers Cam's hand reached out and caught her arm.

'Let me go!'

'Joanne, please. . .'

'What?' She whirled to face him, glaring at him with as much dignity as she could muster. 'What do you want?'

'To apologise.'

'Well, I don't accept.' She swung her streaming hair out of her eyes. 'I quit, Cam Maddon. I refuse to work for a boorish oaf who thinks he can treat me exactly as he chooses. There is plenty of demand for doctors in this country—I don't have to put up with you.'

'Joanne. . .'

'I'm leaving.' She wrenched her arm out of his grasp and started up the beach towards her clothes. 'This morning, if I can.'

'To go where?' he demanded of her retreating back.

'Back to Melbourne. Back where I can have some peace to sit back and consider some decent medical positions.'

'And where does that leave Barbara and Wayne?'

Joanne whirled to face him. 'Oh, isn't that considerate of you?' Her voice was tinged with sarcasm. 'You needn't worry. Jobs aren't so hard to find that I won't have one and be gone before their baby's due. I have a fortnight.'

'You don't.'

'Pardon?'

'I had a phone call just before I came down to the beach. Barbara was safely delivered of a fine son last night.'

For a moment, Joanne's anger fell away. Her eyes softened and moistened. 'Oh, that's lovely. Oh, what good news!'

'So you see, you can't scurry back to your dreary little bolthole.'

'What? Oh, no, I suppose I can't.' She shook her head vaguely, still caught in the delight of the news. Barbara was her dearest friend.

'And so?'

Joanne forced her attention back to the man in front of her, watching her with a slightly puzzled look on his face. She shrugged. 'I don't see what I do is any of your business, Mr Maddon. You're right, though—I won't go back to my house. I can well afford alternative accommodation for a few weeks.'

'Joanne.' Once again Cam caught her hands. Joanne looked disdainfully down at them and he allowed them to fall. 'I would like you to reconsider.'

'Why on earth should I reconsider?'

'Look. . .' He ran a hand wearily through his damp hair. 'I really did come here to apologise. I behaved, as you say, like a boorish oaf. After you left last night I did some hard thinking. The thing is,' he paused and then continued as if fighting for words, 'I've been through a personally harrowing experience. I loved my wife, and she left me.' He held up a hand to stop Joanne interjecting. 'I know—it's nothing to do with you. It is, though, in that since Lindy left me I've been projecting her personality on any single woman I meet.'

'You mean when you kissed me last night you were thinking of Lindy?'

'Something like that.' He gave a mirthless laugh. 'I'm sorry. Stupid, unprofessional, unpardonable. Can you please accept that I've been overworked and emotionally overwrought? Lindy's arrival yesterday was just the final straw.'

'And this morning you suddenly realised that you're still overworked and where the hell are you going to get another assistant.'

'Something like that,' he admitted.

Joanne looked up at him for a long moment. She would have to be stupid, she thought, to agree to stay. Her eyes dropped and were caught, mesmerised by the fine dark hairs on his chest. She had a suddenly overwhelming urge to run her fingers from the hollow in his throat down to the deep crease at his narrowed waist. She gave herself a mental shake. This was a man who had sworn not to go near his ex-wife, and yet had gone to see her within an hour of her arriving on the island. This was a man who had admitted kissing Joanne only because he was thinking of Lindy.

And yet. . . The dark eyes held her, locked with hers in a message of gentle reassurance. Confused, she abruptly turned away, stooping to retrieve her sarong. By the time she had twisted it around herself and secured it firmly above her breasts she had herself under control.

'All right,' she muttered, 'I'll stay. But from here on in our relationship is purely professional. If you lay one finger on me I'm on the next plane out of here.'

'Agreed,' he replied gravely.

'And my personal appearance is my business.'

He nodded.

'Fine.' Joanne jammed on her sandals and stalked off down the track.

CHAPTER SEVEN

WITH her personal relationship with Cam Maddon sorted out, as she thought, Joanne found the remaining facets of her change in lifestyle interesting and rewarding. There was more than enough work on the island to support two doctors, although as Cam explained, it would get quieter in the summer months. At the moment, with winter at its bleakest in the southern states, the tourist season was at its peak, with every tourist facility booked out. Joanne's surgeries consisted of every third patient requiring treatment for sunburn.

She found it difficult to be sympathetic in the face of blatant carelessness. Often, children were brought in by their mothers for treatment of sunburn which could only have been gained by long hours of unprotected exposure. On Joanne's third day on the island she was called on to treat a six-week-old baby which had been left to sleep in a pram under a tree and 'the sun moved, Doctor'. It certainly had! The infant had been wearing a singlet and a nappy, and its arms, legs and little face were blistered raw. As Joanne set up a drip to restore fluids to the little body she shook her head in disbelief. This mother had learned a hard lesson, but she knew it wasn't the last case she would see on the island.

Cam was checking on Chris Tanner while Joanne was working on her little sunburn victim. He came across to see and grimaced.

'Poor little devil. He's not going to be too happy with the world for a while.'

Joanne shook her head. 'I can't believe the sunburn I'm seeing. It's like an epidemic.' She was trying to find a vein in the tiny hand.

'I know,' Cam agreed. 'The people from the south here on holiday are the worst. They come for ten days and think they've failed if they don't go home with a tan. Often we get people quite dangerously ill, like this little one here.'

He handed her the padded board used for immobilising the tiny arm. 'Not that the locals are any more sensible in the long run,' he continued. He was passing the tape to Joanne as she needed it. 'It's impossible to convince them that a tan is not a sign of glowing health. In consequence, if you live in Queensland you've got almost a hundred per cent chance of getting skin cancer—or worse. The melanoma rate is far higher than it should be. Yet I can still walk along the beach at the height of the midday heat and see perhaps one person in ten wearing a hat. I wish I could bring them in here and show them Mrs Tucker in Room Seventeen, suffering secondaries from a melanoma on her leg. She's got weeks to live, and her daughter comes to visit with the deepest tan I've ever seen. She must spend every available moment working on it.'

Joanne nodded absently. Her attention was taken with the condition of the little boy in the crib below. She wished he would cry. The few little noises he'd made since she'd seen him had been feeble sounds of distress, rather than the full-throated wail of a hungry baby. She looked down at him worriedly.

'He'll be OK.' Joanne looked up to find Cam watching her with eyes that were both amused and concerned. 'He's a fine, strong lad. Once you've restored his fluids he's going to let the world know how much he's hurting. Then, if you like, you can send him home to his mother and let her pay the penalty of her foolishness with a few sleepless nights.'

Joanne smiled but shook her head. 'I won't do that to her. She's a first-time mum and is just appalled at what's happened. Matron's arranged for her to stay here while he's in.'

Cam nodded and left her to it. Joanne watched his broad back retreating down the corridor. She was on duty tonight, so Cam was free, but as she'd passed the sister's station a few minutes ago Joanne had noted his scrawled message letting them know where he could be contacted. It was the large international-standard hotel out on the headland, the obvious place where Lindy would be staying.

Joanne hadn't seen much of Tom over the last few days and guessed that he too would be spending time getting to know his mother. She'd met him in the corridor that morning, dressed in his school clothes.

'I can't stop,' he'd called as he hurried past. 'Mrs Bird drives the school bus and she gets crabby if I'm late. I wanted to come and visit you last night, but Dad said I had to visit her instead.' He had thrown Joanne a wave and dashed over to join a couple of other youngsters waiting at the end of the hospital drive.

It didn't sound as if Tom was enthralled with the beautiful Lindy.

And what of his father? Cam had admitted that he'd loved her. Was that love still alive, waiting to be rekindled? Joanne told herself over and over that it was none of her business and she wasn't interested, but still the question kept niggling at the recesses of her mind. Why had Lindy come? Was she regretting her foolishness of five years ago?

It didn't matter, Joanne told herself firmly for the third time that afternoon, and she turned back to her little patient.

Matron Wheeler came in as Joanne finished. 'Are you eating here tonight, dear? Dinner's being served now.'

Joanne smiled her acknowledgement. She would like to start cooking her own meals, but as yet there hadn't been time for her to investigate the island's shops. The hospital fare was simple and homey, much as Joanne had cooked for her mother in the past. She was itching to try some interesting cooking, an authentic Indian curry, or perhaps even Japanese sushi with the wonderful range of fresh fish available on the island. Most of this sort of food she'd only read about. It was frustrating to be finally on her own and still have to eat the standard hospital meat and three vegies.

It was a good way to meet the hospital staff, though. Meals in the big hospital kitchen were a convivial affair, with much good-natured joking and chivvying. Mrs Robb, the cook, surveyed the staff with a motherly eye.

'Eh, I'm missing Tom,' she confessed to them tonight.

'Where is he?' one of the nurses asked.

'He's with 'is mum,' Mrs Robb retorted. 'Which is only right and proper. But it just doesn't seem right without him.'

'He told me you all looked after him,' Joanne said curiously. 'Is that true?'

'Course it is,' said Mrs Robb expansively. 'We're his family.'

'It's almost true,' Matron Wheeler explained. 'Cam brought Tom here when he was just a baby. The hospital had been without a doctor for nearly six months and we were desperate. Cam's application stipulated that he was only interested in a position if it could include live-in child care. The hospital board approached the staff and we've taken over from there. The door through to Tom's bedroom is just through the other side of the kitchen. Mrs Robb does most of the work involved when his father is busy, like dressing him and putting him to bed. He eats with us and, when his father's out at night, the nursing staff treat Tom's room as they would a patient's room, except,' she said thoughtfully, 'they check it rather more often. It's an unusual arrangement, but it's meant the island's had the services of a more than competent doctor for over four years now.

'Besides which,' she smiled self-consciously, 'we'd all be heartbroken if we lost Tom.' Then, smiling maliciously at the two young nurses at the end of the table, she added her final words. 'Or his dad.'

The girls blushed, and Joanne grinned. It had not taken her long to realise that, as well as being universally liked, Cam Maddon was regarded as the most eligible bachelor on the island.

'It's all very well saying we'd be heartbroken, but the truth is we just may have to face losing them,' Mrs Robb retorted. 'Leastways, that's the way I figure it if that young madam who's Tom's mother has her way. Since she's been on the island the pair of them have either been over at her hotel or she's been on the phone wanting to know when they'll be there. She means to have him again.'

'You don't know that,' Matron rebuked mildly.

Mrs Robb sniffed. The matter was clearly settled.

Joanne left the friendly crowd in the kitchen and

made her way back to her flat. The evening stretched ahead of her. She would have liked to go to the cove for another swim—she'd been there every morning since she arrived and couldn't get enough of the glorious sea—but with Cam gone for the evening she felt restricted. In an emergency she was on duty. She also felt vaguely uneasy about her little sunburn patient. She had done everything she could for him, but she intended to stay close.

The magazines she had taken from the hospital waiting-room did not hold her for long, and after a while she made herself a cup of coffee and went out on the veranda to drink it. The night sister found her there half an hour later.

'We've got a patient in Casualty, Dr Tynon. Could you come?'

'Sure.' Glad of something happening, Joanne followed her back through the darkened corridors.

The man sitting on the examination couch was in his thirties, Joanne guessed, tall, fair and gangly. He wore thick glasses through which he was gloomily surveying a deep gash on his foot. He looked up as Joanne entered.

'Good evening,' Joanne smiled. 'What have you been doing to yourself?' She moved to examine the foot as she spoke. The wound was deep and ragged, running across under the arch and around to the back of his heel. 'Ouch!' she said in sympathy.

'You're telling me,' he said mournfully. 'For the first few minutes after I did it I was concentrating on stopping the bleeding and hardly felt it. Now the bleeding's stopped it's hurting like you wouldn't believe.'

Joanne nodded, intent on the wound.

'It needs stitching?' the man said anxiously, and she smiled.

'Just a few,' she said reassuringly. About twenty, by the look of it, but she wasn't going to go into details with this obviously stressed patient. 'If you could just lie down, Mr. . .?' She stopped on a query.

'Langdon,' he said, lowering his head gratefully back on to the pillows. 'William Langdon. And it's Dr rather than Mr.'

'Dr?' Joanne raised her eyebrows in surprise. From the way he was reacting to his cut she hadn't thought blood and gore was an everyday occurrence for him.

'Oh, not a doctor of medicine.' He gave a weak laugh. 'God forbid! I'm a palaeontologist.'

Joanne nodded intelligently. 'That's very nice for you. I used to collect stamps myself.'

He smiled. 'Good try. Ouch!' This as Joanne gently bathed the area around the cut, looking closely to see if there was dirt in the wound. There was sand, she could see, and perhaps deeper debris.

'OK,' Joanne sighed. 'Relieve my ignorance. What does a palaeontologist do?'

'Studies fossils.'

'Dinosaur bones?'

'Well, if I ever came across any dinosaur bones, I'd study them. They're a bit thin on the ground hereabouts. Actually, I'm here studying the coral.'

'The coral?' Joanne queried in surprise. 'Coral's not a fossil.'

'That's where you're wrong.' Dr Langdon shifted uneasily at Joanne's probing, and she looked up in concern. It was going to be difficult getting enough local anaesthetic in to do the stitching as it should be done. She looked down again at the deepest part of the cut. It really needed subcutaneous stitches, stitches below the level of the outer skin.

Dr Langdon's voice assumed the tone of a professor teaching rather junior students.

'The magnificently coloured coral which is such a tourist attraction for this island is made of continuous skeleton secreted by marine polyps over millions of years.'

Joanne looked up in surprise. He sounded for all the world as if he were addressing a lecture theatre full of students rather than herself. Then she realised that he was not even looking at her. His gaze was on the ceiling, and his lecture was his method of 'biting the bullet'. She encouraged him, throwing in the odd question. As he proceeded to tell her the eighteen-million-year history of the coral she finished her cleaning.

'Wriggle your toes for me,' she demanded, cutting across his discourse.

He looked vaguely offended, but obliged.

'Can you feel this? And this? What am I doing now?' His responses to her tests were all positive. At least there appeared to be no nerve damage.

'So how did you manage to give yourself this cut?' she asked. 'Standing on the coral?'

'I wouldn't be so stupid,' he said indignantly. 'I always take the greatest care when I'm diving.'

'Well?' Joanne demanded. 'You must have done it somehow.'

'On the beach,' he explained. 'As I said, I wear protective gear when I'm diving. I'd finished for the day and was pulling the dinghy up on to the beach. I should have kept my protective gear on. Some stupid idiot had left a broken bottle on the beach and the tide had covered it with a thin layer of sand.'

Joanne frowned. Broken glass. She peered again at the wound. There was no way she could exclude the possibility of glass remaining in the wound without extensive probing.

'OK.' She straightened. 'Dr Langdon, I'm going to have to really clean this cut out. It's chock-full of sand and maybe also broken glass. As well as that I'm going to have to pull it together in a couple of layers. It's very deep.' Her patient's pallor was growing more marked as she spoke. There was clearly a limit to how much biting the bullet his constitution could take.

'I think,' she continued gently, 'that it would be a good idea if I did it under a general anaesthetic. It would mean you'd have to stay in overnight, but really, I could do a better job of cleaning it and you'd undergo much less discomfort.'

William Langdon's colour flooded back. Clearly his relief was heartfelt.

'I. . .' He coughed and started again. 'Well, if you think it best, Doctor. I have to accept your advice.'

Joanne smiled. 'Very wise.'

If Joanne was to give a general anaesthetic she needed Cam. She left the night sister preparing her nervous patient and found a phone. After about a dozen rings, Lindy answered.

'He's off duty,' came Lindy's terse response after Joanne had introduced herself and asked to speak to Cam.

'I know,' Joanne explained patiently. 'However, I need to give a general anaesthetic, and for that we need two doctors.'

'You mean you want him to leave? Now? Can't it wait till the morning?' Her voice expressed incredulity at the impudence of someone interrupting her evening.

Joanne gritted her teeth, but before she could find words to reply Cam came on the phone.

'What's the problem?'

Briefly, Joanne outlined the situation, feeling exceedingly uncomfortable.

'I'll be right over. Fifteen minutes.' In the background Joanne could hear Lindy's expostulation.

He was in the hospital in less than that, striding down the corridor to the sister's station bearing the sleeping Tom in his arms. The sister came forward and relieved him of his burden. This was a routine obviously long established.

The operation was straightforward. Cam gave the anaesthetic, deferring to Joanne. He resisted her demur.

'Don't be silly—he's your patient. You have the skills to stitch this.'

'If I could be sure there isn't nerve damage. . .'

'In all probability there's not,' he replied calmly. 'All the signs are good. Besides, you know how to check as well as I do.'

Joanne did, but she found operating under Cam's watchful eye disconcerting.

As the sleeping Dr Langdon was wheeled back to his ward, Joanne was left with Cam. He seemed in no hurry to disrobe, and she found herself growing flustered. Outside a purely professional role, this man unsettled her badly.

'I'm sorry I interrupted your evening,' she said awkwardly.

'That's OK.' He leaned back against the sink, watching her wash her hands. 'I was ready for an interruption.'

What did that mean? Joanne cast a quick glance up at him, but his face was calm and inscrutable.

'Would you like to come back to my flat and have coffee?'

The words were out before Joanne could stop herself. She could have bitten her tongue off. What on earth was she doing?

'Yes, please.' The dark eyes showed a hint of amusement.

They walked together through the hushed hospital. Every nerve in Joanne's body was alight to the presence of the man beside her. What sort of power did the man possess to make her feel like this? She gave herself a mental shake, trying to dispel the aura of unreality. The tension remained.

He seated himself on one of her big sitting-room chairs while she made coffee, and gazed round appreciatively.

'You've made this very pleasant.'

All Joanne had done was to fill the room with flowers which the hospital gardener had assured her would never be missed from the garden and arrange her personal photographs and books about the room. It was true, though. She had made the room look comfortable and inviting.

'More homey than your apartment,' she commented, and then shook her head. She had no right to criticise.

Cam took the coffee she was offering and looked up at her. 'I take it you don't approve of my austere living arrangements.'

'Well, it doesn't seem the sort of place I'd like to call home if I were five years old,' Joanne defended herself.

Cam nodded acknowledgement. 'I know. I guess I've always thought of this place as being a temporary home.'

'Until you and Lindy get back together.'

It was out. Said. Now there was only silence.

Cam nodded finally. 'I guess I've always thought that,' he said heavily.

'Well.' Joanne tried for a cheerful note. It sounded odd, almost offensive. 'Now she's back. For good?'

Cam looked slowly up at her, but Joanne had the impression he was looking straight through her, at some distant, longed-for object. He closed his eyes briefly, then pushed his coffee-mug back on to the table and rose.

'Thank you for the coffee, Joanne.'

'My pleasure.' Joanne's voice was an uncertain whisper. She walked with him to the door.

He pushed the door to the veranda open, and then stopped. For a long moment he stayed motionless. Joanne stood beside the door, waiting.

Cam turned. His hands came up to cup her wondering face. Very lightly he dropped a kiss on her tilted lips.

'Thank you, Joanne. Goodnight.'

He was gone, striding across the dew-damp lawn to his home and his sleeping son. Joanne was left in a torrent of uncertainty. She was sure of only one thing. She was hopelessly, irrevocably and totally in love with Cam Maddon.

CHAPTER EIGHT

JOANNE woke early after a troubled night's sleep. For a while she lay watching the early morning light filter into the room. She glanced at her watch. Six o'clock. Too early for her day to start, yet she was too wide awake to return to sleep.

Ten minutes later she was immersed in the glistening water of her cove. The water shook away the last remnants of sleep as nothing else could. She swam as if driven, from one side of the little bay to the other, again and again in tireless rhythm. The turmoil in her mind eased as she pushed herself to her limit. Her lithe body cut through the water like a dolphin, streamlined and sleek. For a while she could forget the tensions and conflicts surrounding her and glory in the beauty of the ocean, the power and strength of her body.

Finally she had to stop. Physically she had driven herself to the limit. As she pulled herself up on to her favourite ledge she caught a fleeting movement from the beach. By the time she was on the ledge and was able to see the beach clearly, the sand was deserted. She knew, though. Joanne shook her head in gentle derision at herself, but the certainty remained. Cam had been watching her.

He was nowhere to be seen when Joanne did her ward rounds. It was still early.

To her relief her tiny sunburn patient was showing definite signs of improvement. He was awake as she entered the ward and was letting everyone within

83

earshot know he was not happy about his condition, not to mention his empty tummy. When Joanne left he was settled on his young mother's breast, choosing to ignore the pain of having his suburn touched in his quest for breakfast. By the look of his mother's swollen eyes she had been suffering almost as much as her son.

William Langdon was also tucking into a hearty breakfast. He looked up in pleasure as Joanne entered.

'Good morning.' His greeting was somewhat muffled due to a mouth full of bacon.

'Well,' Joanne grinned, 'you don't appear to be suffering.'

He shook his head. 'This place is wonderful. I wouldn't mind a week's stay.'

'And here I was ready to let you go home after breakfast.' Joanne frowned. 'You need to develop more symptoms if we're to justify a hospital bed. Or another operation? How do you feel about a tonsillectomy?'

William held up his hands in mock horror. 'Not for me, thanks, Doctor. Bacon and eggs I can take in any quantity you care to dish out, but I've heard nasty rumours that removal of tonsils involves administration of jelly and ice-cream, and I've never been a man for jelly. If you don't mind, I think I'll stay attached to my tonsils. I guess I'll just have to take myself off.'

Joanne walked to the end of the bed and picked up his chart. His obs were nicely normal. She smiled up at him. She was satisfied with the job she had done on his foot, but, in addition to the pleasure of having performed a task well, she also felt that this man could be a friend.

'Actually we're not quite as ruthless as I'm making out,' she said gently. 'You're going to have to stay right off your foot for ten days. If you're not in a position to do that at home, then we'll keep you here.'

'Ten days?' His voice was horror-filled.

'Ten days. I took a great deal of trouble over those stitches and I don't want you splitting them.'

He pushed his glasses down his nose and looked at her fiercely. 'What about a week?'

'Ten days. Not negotiable.'

'But. . .'

'Sorry.'

He lay back against his pillows and eyed her in dismay. The movement stirred his foot and he grimaced.

'Hurting?' Joanne picked up his chart. 'You're just about due for some pain relief. You're probably going to have to take something for a couple of days. It's a really nasty cut; you're lucky not to have any permanent damage. Now, would you like to stay on here?'

'No.' He shook his head slowly. 'All my stuff is back at the hotel, including my computer. I've probably got enough raw data ready for analysis to keep me happy for a week.'

'Ten days.'

He grinned and held up a hand in defeat. 'OK—ten days.'

'And you can be looked after there?'

He smiled. 'All I have to do is dial room service.'

'Where are you staying?'

'The Coral Sands.'

'Good grief!' The Coral Sands was the hotel where Lindy was staying, the plushest establishment on the island.

'I know.' William assumed an air of martyrdom.

'What we academics have to put up with in the name of scientific enquiry is something horrible.'

Joanne nodded sympathetically. 'And I suppose it's all funded by us poor taxpayers.'

He grinned. 'Well, at least you know your money is being appreciated.'

'Humph!'

Joanne was checking his foot as she spoke. The wound itself she left covered. 'This seems fine. I'll get Sister to find you a pair of crutches and organise the ambulance to drop you back to the hotel later this morning. I want to see your foot in a few days. I've cleaned it pretty thoroughly, but there's always the possibility of infection. If you like I'll drop in to the hotel on Thursday.' Joanne had a small car, provided by the hospital.

'I can get a taxi and come here.'

'It's no bother,' Joanne assured him. 'I'm new to the island and house calls give me a chance to explore.'

He eyed her over his glasses. 'By Thursday I could be just about at the end of my tolerance for my own company. What if I included dinner in the deal?'

'Lovely.' Joanne nodded inwardly to herself. What she needed was to get away from this hospital. Light diversion provided by William Langdon would be perfect.

The rest of the morning passed peacefully enough. Joanne's clinics were usually quiet, mostly consisting of tourists with trivial complaints. The permanent island residents preferred to use Cam, the doctor they knew and trusted, and Joanne had to suppress a twinge of jealousy at the sight of his list for the morning. It would be nice to treat something other than sunburn.

She gained her wish with the last patient for the morning. As she emerged from the surgery to call in the next patient, Joanne found Lindy waiting for her.

Joanne stood at the door and waited as Lindy entered. The woman was almost inappropriately dressed, she thought, in this casual holiday resort. Her wide silk trousers in a splash of tropical hues and her near-translucent silk blouse would have been more at home on a catwalk in London rather than in a doctor's surgery at a beach resort. Joanne was inexplicably glad of her white coat, her badge of professionalism.

'What can I do for you?' she returned to her chair behind her desk.

Lindy carefully seated herself in the chair opposite. There was silence in the room while she adjusted the folds of silk to her satisfaction. Finally she raised her eyes to Joanne's.

'I'd like to talk to you about my son, if I may.'

'Tom?'

'Thomas. Yes.'

Joanne looked at her curiously. 'What would you like to talk about?'

Lindy smiled. 'I'd just like to clear up a couple of small queries about his medical condition. How fit would you say he was?'

Joanne's forehead creased in surprise. What was this all about? 'As far as I know he's a normal, healthy little boy,' she responded finally. 'I'm not his doctor, though.'

'But that awful brace. . .'

'I assume it's an attempt to correct the problem with his foot.' Joanne hesitated and looked at the card in front of her. Mrs Maddon. In name at least, Lindy was still Cam's wife. 'Mrs Maddon, I'm afraid I can tell you very little about your son. He's not my patient. All I know of his leg or his general medical condition is what he's told me himself and what's obvious by my own observation.'

'I see.' Was it Joanne's imagination, or had Lindy relaxed? Was this some sort of test? There was an undercurrent of tension in the room that was almost palpable. For some reason Joanne found herself keeping guard, watching for some sort of threat that she couldn't put a name to. She gave herself a mental shake. Given her emotional involvement with Cam she was bound to feel this way about Lindy.

'Do you think it's necessary that he keep wearing the brace?' Lindy asked. Her voice was light, but her eyes were watchful.

Joanne picked up a pen and tapped it lightly on the pad in front of her. She was buying time, trying to sort out what Lindy wanted from her. There was nothing she could say but the truth, regardless of what Lindy wanted to hear.

'I'm afraid I'm in no position to form an opinion, Mrs Maddon. I've never even examined Tom. Even if I did, I'm afraid it's an area where I'd be referring him for specialist advice. I don't have the experience to treat him myself.'

'So you'd agree to the idea of his seeing a specialist?' The response was fast—too fast.

'I'm sure he has seen someone.' Joanne frowned in puzzlement. 'Cam wouldn't be treating him himself.'

'Mr Maddon,' Lindy's voice dropped its honeyed warmth, 'has informed me that Tom is being treated by some person in Cairns.' Her voice left Joanne in no doubt as to what she thought of that idea. 'I would like

Thomas to see the best specialist available inter-
nationally. Am I right in imagining you would have no
objection to that?'

'It's none of my business.'

'On the contrary.' Lindy's voice was controlled,
carefully working towards her goal. 'As you're the only
doctor on this island who's not related to Thomas, I
need you to verify that Thomas is fit to travel and
requires specialist treatment.' She curled one hand up
to inspect the flawless surface of her manicured nails.
'I have had legal advice that unless there's any absolute
reason why Thomas cannot travel then medical treatment clearly unavailable here should not be denied to
him.'

'You want to take him back to England?' Joanne
sank back into her chair. At least she knew now what
Lindy was after.

'Of course.' Lindy flashed her a brilliant smile. 'Well,
he is my son, and England is my home.'

'You're going to make him very unhappy if you
manage to take him away from his father.'

'Who said anything about taking him away from his
father?' Lindy's eyes widened in polite surprise. 'I
would imagine, if it's necessary for Thomas to return
to England, his father will also come.'

'You want Cam to go too?'

'Of course.'

Joanne's pen, she discovered, had made a hole in
the pad in front of her. She crumpled the ruined sheet
of paper and thrust it into her drawer. When she raised
her eyes Lindy was watching her speculatively.

'There's really no need for any discussion, my dear,'
she said kindly. 'As long as you can verify that Thomas
is fit to travel that's all I need from you.'

'Why would such a verification be necessary?'

Lindy smiled. 'Well, let's just say I'm covering myself in the eventuality that Mr Maddon doesn't see the necessity for further specialist opinion as clearly as we do.'

'As you do,' Joanne said bluntly, and Lindy inclined her head in polite acknowledgement.

'As you like.' Her tone as bored. 'As I said, though, I have had legal advice. My decision to have him seen by a specialist of international repute would receive favourable consideration from a court of law, in the eventuality of his father being foolish enough to protest.' She rose. 'In the next few days you'll be receiving a letter from a firm of English lawyers asking you to verify what you've just told me.'

'I can't,' Joanne said decisively. 'There is no way I can respond to any medical query about Tom without having examined him.'

'You will have.' It was the same flat, uninterested voice. Clearly Lindy had achieved what she had come for. She moved towards the door, and Joanne stood up. 'His father can't refuse my request for a doctor to see him. With only Cam and yourself on the island, you, my dear, are it.' She gave a faint smile. 'By the way, I'm sorry if my return has interrupted any little plans you might have laid yourself with regard to my husband.'

Joanne stopped her movement towards the door. Her face must have registered pure shock. Lindy gave a gentle laugh.

'I do have eyes, you know,' she smiled. 'I do think you could do better for yourself than to fall for a married man.'

Joanne took a deep breath. 'I have heard that

Cameron Maddon has been without a wife for a very long time,' she said softly.

The other girl's smile didn't falter. 'Well, I guess it's true that I haven't been around for a while,' she agreed. 'I intend to remedy that.'

Joanne nodded. 'By forcing them back to England.'

'Oh, I don't think much force will be involved,' Lindy said lightly. 'He's been trying for so long, you see, to turn me into a perfect mother. How can he now deny my very natural longing for my son?' She laughed. 'After I get the child in hospital for tests and Cam back on my territory, well. . .' She broke off and gave Joanne her friendliest smile. 'Enough. I'm keeping you from your work. I'll see you tomorrow, Dr Tynon, when I bring Thomas for his examination.'

She was gone, leaving Joanne rigid with shock and anger.

Joanne didn't see Cam for the rest of the afternoon, which was just as well considering the turmoil in her head. After dinner she took a long hard walk along the road near the hospital. Having calmed down to the point where she thought she had herself under control, she returned to the flat and placed a phone call to Melbourne. She needed to talk to someone, and there was only Barbara. It was odd dialling the number she knew so well. Barbara's voice came down the line as clearly as if she were a block away rather than over a thousand miles. Her familiar voice was balm to Joanne's tangled nerves, and she listened with pleasure to Barbara's account of the perfection of her tiny son.

'I wish I could see him,' she said finally.

'So fly down for the baptism. I suppose you and Cam

won't both be able to come? That's a bother. You will be his godmother, won't you?'

'Of course,' Joanne agreed warmly.

'Wayne was thinking of asking Cam to be godfather. Do you think he'd do it?'

'I don't know.' Joanne shook her head dubiously. 'You'd have to ask him. He may be returning to England.'

'England?'

'Lindy's come back.'

There was silence on the other end of the phone, and then Barbara uttered an expletive.

'Pardon?'

'You didn't hear that. It's the poor connection or something. Drat, though. Wayne said she might.'

'How did he know?' Joanne asked curiously. 'I don't think Cam was expecting her.'

'Then Cam doesn't have a clue about what Wayne has suspected all along.'

'Which is?'

Barbara gave a little sigh of pleasure. 'Oh, it's lovely to be able to gossip with you again! Now you won't ever tell Cam that Wayne said this. . .'

'Cross my heart.'

Barbara's delicious gurgle sounded down the line. 'Well,' Joanne could just imagine her settling more comfortably into the chair beside the phone, 'Wayne's theory is that Lindy married Cam for his money.'

'I didn't think he was wealthy.'

'Well, neither has he been. Cam's father, however, seemed to own half of New South Wales. It was common knowledge that he was disgustingly wealthy. Cam was the only son. Lindy met Cam just after his father died and it was generally thought that Cam had inherited millions.'

'And he hadn't?'

'Well, according to the grapevine, Cam's father had left a will which had been made before Cam was born, leaving everything to his wife, Cam's mother. There was no way Cam could touch the capital until his mother died.'

'But if it was out of date, surely Cam could have contested it?'

'Apparently he didn't want to. His mother would have deeded money over to him, but he couldn't see the point. He was making a good salary and he preferred to leave things as they were.'

'Lindy wouldn't have been happy with that.'

'I suppose not. You know the lady—I don't. But Wayne was of the same opinion, and he wasn't really surprised when he heard that Lindy had left. And he won't be surprised when I tell him Lindy is back.'

'Why not?'

'Cam's mother died a couple of months ago.'

Joanne's surgery list the next morning was the usual list of unknowns. This morning, however, there was one exception. The first patient for the morning was Thomas Maddon. Joanne handed the list back to Maree, the receptionist, and eyed Cam's closed surgery door with misgiving. It was early still, and the first of the booked patients had not yet arrived. Taking a deep breath, she stepped over and knocked on the door.

'Come in.'

Cam was seated at the desk, his head bent over paperwork. He glanced up briefly as she entered, but, as he saw who it was, applied himself again to his writing.

'Yes?' His tone was curt.

'I see you've booked Tom in to see me,' Joanne said hesitantly.

'Lindy has booked Tom in to see you,' he responded harshly. 'I assume you know all about it.'

Joanne bit her lip and took a deep breath. This wasn't going to be easy. 'Suppose,' she said softly, 'you tell me what I'm supposed to do.'

Cam finally looked up. 'Oh, that's easy. Lindy intends to claim Tom and you're going to help her with all the legal niceties.'

'Is that what she says?'

He rubbed a hand wearily through his dark hair. 'Of course it is. She's just been skirting around the issue since she came to the island, but she finally told me last night. She wants Tom back in England where she can see him whenever she wants. She'll use his medical problems to force my hand if I don't agree.' His eyes met Joanne's in bleak acceptance. 'I can't blame her. She is his mother.'

Joanne looked silently at him for a long moment. There seemed to be little anger, no urge to fight. As far as Cam was concerned Lindy's motives were purely love and desire for her son. Did he really have no idea of the complex game she seemed to be playing?

'Does she want him back to live with her?' Joanne spoke cautiously.

He shook his head. 'No, I gather that wouldn't be possible. She has to support herself with her work. Since she left us she's had a fairly difficult time.'

As the designer clothes show, Joanne thought nastily. She bit back the comment. Instead she kept her voice carefully neutral.

'Would you consider returning to England, then?'

There was a long silence, stretching out interminably. It was as if something had to be said that neither of them wanted to hear. Finally Cam looked up and met Joanne's eyes.

'I'd have to.'

Joanne nodded, her eyes not leaving Cam's. The desolation descending on her was frightening, as if a part of her were being wrenched physically away. Lindy was going to have it all her own way.

'Well, I don't really need to see Tom, then, do I?' she asked bleakly. 'It sounds as if you've already come to a decision.'

Silence again. Cam broke their gaze and looked down at the pad in front of him. 'Jo, I haven't made a final decision. The fact that you'd be the only doctor left on the island would have to come into any decision I make.' His voice was heavy, loaded with sadness and regret. Joanne felt an almost unbearable urge to reach out and smooth the lines of fatigue running across his forehead.

'If we have to go back to England, then we must, but I'll delay as long as I can,' he continued. 'Lindy walked out on us.' His mouth twisted in a cynical line. 'The decision was hers. Even though she wants us to leave tomorrow I'll be able to delay for a while. Tom hasn't got a passport—that'll take time. She won't be able to argue unless,' he looked up at her again, 'unless you provide her with medical ammunition by stating that Tom needs urgent attention.'

'Of course I won't,' Joanne said savagely. 'Do you think I'm working for your wife?'

'She is not,' Cam stated flatly, 'my wife. Our divorce has been through for nearly four years, and since that time she's had at least one other husband. I assume she's only using my name for Tom's sake.'

'Or because that's what she wants again,' said Joanne. To her horror she could hear bitterness in her words.

'Joanne. . .' Cam rose and reached out a hand to her. To her horror, she felt tears well up behind her eyelids. She willed herself to turn away, but her body disobeyed her. She was locked, mesmerised, with tears slipping unheeded down her cheeks.

'Mr Maddon.' The receptionist's voice crackled through the intercom as Cam started towards her. 'Mrs Harrison has arrived for her appointment, and Mrs Maddon is here with Tom for Dr Tynon.'

Cam stopped. His eyes still on Joanne's face, he leaned to speak into the intercom. 'Thanks, Maree. Give us a minute.'

'I. . . I'll go.' Joanne wrenched herself around to face the door.

'Joanne?'

'Yes?' She didn't turn back.

He hesitated. When finally he spoke his voice was devoid of expression. 'Tom is being looked after by Richard Crossley in Cairns. His credentials in paediatric orthopaedics are excellent. Tom's last appointment was two months ago when he had his current brace fitted. If you need any information I'm sure he'll oblige.'

'Thank you.' Joanne turned the handle and made her escape.

Joanne's examination of Tom was straightforward. She spent the time verifying what she had known all along, that Tom's leg was being given the very best treatment

Mills & Boon

Discover
FREE BOOKS
AND
FREE GIFTS
From Mills & Boon

**As a special introduction to
Mills & Boon Romances we will send you:**

FOUR FREE Mills & Boon Romances plus a FREE
TEDDY and MYSTERY GIFT when you return this card.

**But first - just for fun - see if you can find and circle four
hidden words in the puzzle.**

R	D	A	V	R	Y	B	X	N	M
B	O	O	K	N	C	A	S	P	Y
Z	G	M	N	B	U	L	T	R	S
R	T	N	A	N	E	F	T	A	T
D	H	I	A	N	V	K	D	M	E
N	W	L	K	H	C	O	W	S	R
O	C	O	M	U	T	E	D	D	Y
I	L	V	F	L	P	B	I	T	E
F	E	E	J	S	G	I	F	T	P
S	P	N	S	E	T	I	N	R	E

**The hidden
words are:**

MYSTERY
ROMANCE
TEDDY
GIFT

Now turn over to claim your
FREE BOOKS AND GIFTS

Free Books Certificate

Yes! Please send me four specially selected Mills & Boon Romances, together with my FREE Teddy and Mystery Gift. I would also like you to reserve a special Reader Service Subscription for me. Which means that I can go on to enjoy six brand new Romances sent to me each month for just £8.70, postage and packing FREE. If I decide not to subscribe I shall write to you within 10 days. Any FREE books and gifts will remain mine to keep. I understand that I am under no obligation whatsoever - I can cancel or suspend my subscription at any time simply by writing to you. I am over 18 years of age.

4A1R

FREE TEDDY

MYSTERY GIFT

Mrs./Miss./Mr _____

Address _____

_____

_____ Postcode _____

Signature _____

NO
STAMP
NEEDED

Reader Service
FREEPOST
P.O. Box 236
Croydon
Surrey CR9 9EL

possible. Having just come from one of the country's major teaching hospitals Joanne had seen other children with Tom's problem and knew that the treatment he was receiving was absolutely standard. She was sure, though, that Lindy would be able to find a medical practitioner somewhere who would swear to have developed a new wonder treatment, and the law would look sympathetically at her wish to use it.

Tom was indignant. 'I thought you were my friend, not my doctor. My doctor's Mr Crossley in Cairns. I'm not sick. We were putting on a play at school this morning and now I've missed it.' He glared at both Lindy and Joanne, and Joanne cringed inwardly. She didn't like being paired with Lindy.

'I guess it's natural that your mum worries about you,' she reassured him. 'After all, she hasn't met Mr Crossley.' She turned to Lindy. 'If you're worried, perhaps I could arrange for you to see him.' It was a faint hope, and she knew before she made the remark what Lindy's response would be.

'The next doctor Thomas sees will be an English one,' Lindy said flatly. 'You'll like coming home with me, won't you, Thomas?'

He looked up from the examination couch at his beautiful mother and eyed her with disdain. 'Home is here.'

'Well. . .' Lindy laughed nervously, and Joanne realised that in the time she had been here she had still not developed any sort of familiarity with the little boy. 'A visit with Daddy and me, then. The sooner the better, I think, don't you agree, Dr Tynon?'

'As far as I can see,' Joanne returned unhelpfully, 'there's no reason for Tom to make the trip at all. I certainly don't see any need for urgency.'

'You can vouch for the fact that there's no medical reason why he shouldn't travel, though, can't you, Dr Tynon?'

'Yes.' There was no way Joanne could avoid giving the girl this much help. She tousled the little boy's hair. 'He's as strong as an ox.'

'You'll write a statement to that effect?'

'If you insist.'

'Thank you, Dr Tynon.' Lindy held out an imperious hand to Tom. 'That's all I need from you.'

She swept out, towing Tom behind her. As they reached the door Tom swung around to give Joanne a last look. His face said it all. 'I thought you were my friend.'

CHAPTER NINE

THE next few days were tense and unhappy. Cam walked around with a face like a thundercloud. Unless he was actually talking to patients he spoke in monosyllables, cutting short any attempts by the staff at usual pleasantries.

'Wow!' one of the junior nurses muttered to Joanne as she recoiled from a blast. 'I knew his wife was back, but if that's what marriage does to you, I'm for being an old maid every time.' She looked down in indignation at the offending hospital corner on the bed. 'Matron hasn't worried about these for years. Why is it suddenly upsetting his lordship that Mr Rowlands can stick his toe out?'

Joanne grimaced sympathetically, but her sympathy really lay with Cam. What was Lindy doing to him? Even if she persuaded him to return to England, could she make him happy?

The staff gossiped mercilessly, and mealtimes were a nightmare for Joanne. She hated the endless speculation. William Langdon's invitation to dinner on Thursday night came as a blessed escape.

She dressed with care. Since she had arrived on the island she had had little opportunity to wear the beautiful clothes she had bought in Melbourne. They were all a bit wasted when she immediately covered anything she put on with a white coat. She spent some time deciding what to wear, enjoying the novelty of being able to choose. A persistent nagging at the back of her mind kept intruding with the thought, I wish it were Cam I was dressing for. She ruthlessly pushed it aside. Tonight was her first night out since she had arrived at the island, and she was going to enjoy herself.

Finally she decided on a startling gold and crimson skirt, a crimson crossover blouse with a back which plunged to nothing and a wide black sash. She stood gazing at the reflection in her mirror with astonishment. Who was this? Finally, she reached up and released the combs holding back her hair. She ran her hand through the riot of curls. The thought came into her mind, I look free.

'Damn Cam Maddon,' she said out loud to her reflection. 'I am going to enjoy myself tonight and I don't intend to think of him all night.'

She felt a little self-conscious walking into the foyer of the Coral Sands. I'm going to have to get myself colour co-ordinated doctor's bags, she thought as the mixed image of her clothes and black bag drew curious glances. It was worth it, though, when she entered William's room and saw his face light up with pleasure. He'd had a lonely and painful few days, she guessed.

'Wow! Do you always do house calls looking like this?'

'The red hides the bloodstains,' she said firmly.

'Oh, great!'

Joanne grinned. 'OK, let's get this over with. On to the bed with you.'

'You have a lovely romantic line, lady.'

She giggled. 'Enough! I'm in a good position to retaliate, remember.'

William groaned and hopped over to the bed. 'You

realise this is not how I usually like to impress my lady
friends. I've gone to a great deal of trouble tonight,
clean shirt and everything, and all you're interested in
is my foot.'

'Just so long as it's clean, is all I care about,' she
agreed gravely. She unwound the dressing carefully.
'Oh, good.'

'OK?'

'Healing nicely.'

'Then about that ten days . . .?'

'Ten days is what I said. Ten days is what I meant.'

With his foot re-dressed they made their way to the
dining-room, William relying heavily on his crutches.
As Joanne had suspected, he proved to be an easy
companion, interested in her work as well as wishing
to tell her about his. He was intensely homesick, she
discovered.

'You won't get up and walk out if I tell you I have a
fiancée in Brisbane?' he asked anxiously.

She laughed. 'No. Why should I? Would she approve
of my being here, though?'

'I told her,' he smiled. 'I've rung her up every day
since the accident. She was delighted I was actually
going to spend some time with another human being.
She says any time I spend away from fossils is time well
spent.'

The evening sped without them really noticing the
time. They were both in the same basket, thought
Joanne as she rose to leave—damnably lonely. William
had an end in view to his isolation. A couple more
weeks and his research would be finished. As for
herself. . . She shook herself mentally. Tonight she
wasn't going to think about it.

Despite her protests William escorted her out to the car. 'Goodnight, Joanne. Thank you for saving my life.'

'You've got to be kidding! I only stitched your foot.'

'If you hadn't come tonight I'd be a splat mark on the pavement underneath my fourth-floor window,' he assured her seriously. 'Or I'd be gone. I very much want to stay and get this finished before heading back to Brisbane, so you've helped me enormously. I tell you what,' he reached down and opened her car door for her, 'by Saturday week my stitches will be out. I've got to do a couple more deep dives. What say you come out with me to the reef? I've got a couple of snorkels and masks. We can do a bit of shallow diving and then you can mind my hose while I go right down.'

'It sounds like fun. Is hose-minding hard?'

'Back-breaking. Bring a novel and some sunscreen.' He bent and kissed her lightly on the cheek. 'Goodnight, Joanne.'

As he stepped back from the car Joanne saw two figures standing behind him on the hotel steps. Cam and Lindy. Her enjoyment of the evening evaporated as if it had never been, and with a shock she recognised the feeling within her. It was pure jealousy. With an effort she forced a smile to William and waved lightly to the couple on the steps before turning her little car away from the hotel, out into the night.

The next few days were busy. Joanne threw herself into her work, using it to keep her mind away from the precarious emotions it was experiencing.

'I'm just naïve,' she told herself crossly. 'Most girls have schoolgirl crushes. Here I am, twenty-eight and no more able to hide my emotions than a schoolgirl.'

She greeted Cam curtly when she saw him, talking to him at a professional level and nothing else.

Her summons for an ultimatum wasn't unexpected. He caught her as they finished a morning surgery.

'Can I see you for a moment, Joanne?' His voice was grave, and she knew what was coming.

'You know I'm going to have to leave,' he said as they seated themselves formally on either side of his desk.

Joanne nodded. She had prepared herself for this and was determined to be briskly businesslike.

'I assumed you would be. When are you going?'

'In a fortnight.'

Joanne's heart lurched sickeningly, but she met his look.

'So that leaves me where you were—looking after the hospital single-handed.' For a moment the thought overwhelmed her, and her eyes must have reflected her panic. Cam rose and walked to the window.

'Well, that's what I wanted to talk to you about. I intend to advertise, and I thought I'd advertise for two doctors. A husband and wife team would be ideal for the island. I've got more chance of getting a response if I advertise the position as such.'

Joanne stood silent for a moment, assimilating what he was telling her. 'So where does that leave me?'

Cam turned and spoke evenly. 'It leaves you doing what you told me you were capable of less than a fortnight ago. Finding another job.'

Joanne sucked in her breath. 'You're sacking me!'

'I'm asking you to resign as soon as we can find replacements.'

'May I ask why?' Joanne's voice was a tight, controlled thread.

Cam continued to look out of the window, watching a nurse push a wheelchair out under the trees.

'I am entitled to know,' Joanne said softly.

'Joanne, this hospital needs doctors who are committed to it.'

'And I'm not?'

'No.'

Joanne took a deep breath. Still Cam remained facing away from her. 'On what grounds are you making that assumption?'

'Oh, for heaven's sake!' He spun round to face her, his face dark with anger. 'Do I have to spell it out? There is no way, Dr Tynon, that you intend to spend any significant length of time at this hospital. You'll be married and off in no time. If I advertise for a doctor and you walk out, where does that leave him?'

'What makes you so sure I'll be married?' Joanne asked through gritted teeth. Keep calm, she told herself fiercely. Keep calm.

Cam laughed, a bitter, goading laugh that made Joanne flinch. 'Just look at you,' he told her. 'You don't dress like that to spend the rest of your life doing medicine. You've been here a fortnight and already you've found yourself a boyfriend. You've checked me out and now you're on to number two.'

'You. . .' Joanne sucked in her breath. She felt as if a bucket of iced water had just been poured over her. 'You chauvinistic, arrogant. . .'

She caught herself. For a moment she closed her eyes, and when she opened them she had regained some composure.

'Mr Maddon, I take it you wish to leave in a fortnight, leaving me to cope until the new medical team that you hope to find can take over from my incompetent care.'

'I didn't say you were incompetent.'

Joanne raised her eyebrows in polite disbelief. 'But, essentially, I have it correct.'

Cam nodded agreement, his eyes expressionless.

'I hate to disappoint you, then,' Joanne went on icily, 'but that scenario appals me and I want no part of it. My contract stipulates a month's trial, and that month is up in a fortnight. I'll leave then.'

'But I'll never get replacements by then!'

'That, Mr Maddon, is your problem and it's you who are going to have to sit it out and wait, not me.'

'Joanne, that's petty.'

'Petty!' Joanne's voice raised incredulously. 'Petty! Who's just sacked a perfectly competent doctor because she dares to look presentable and likes making friends?' She turned and stalked out of the room, slamming the door with all her might behind her.

Joanne's anger carried her through the afternoon. She was booked at the local primary school for a session of routine medical examinations. It's just as well it's not an injection session, she thought ruefully as she listened patiently to the eye chart being read. In my present mood, I'd hurt!

By the time she had finished examining thirty small bodies, much of Joanne's anger had evaporated. She was left with an empty feeling of desolation and loneliness. This had been her first job away from Melbourne, and, no matter how unjust the reason for her failure, she had failed. She glanced at her watch. It was time for dinner at the hospital. She would have to rush if she was to make it.

Halfway back along the narrow, tree-lined road she changed her mind. The hospital kitchen would be oppressive. If Cam had told them of his decision to leave there would be talk of nothing else. Joanne turned her little car off the road and made her way down to the island jetty.

The fishing co-op was situated at the end of the jetty. The elderly lady behind the counter recognised Joanne and greeted her with pleasure. Under the glass counter were rows of scarlet lobsters, cooked and begging to be eaten. Joanne chose a small one and purchased a bottle of mineral water from the vending machine on the wall.

'Are you heading to the beach to eat it?' the woman asked.

'How did you guess?'

'It's a common habit around here, though personally I can't think of anything worse,' the lady smiled. 'Sand is all very well in its place, but that's not in your sandwiches. Picnics are for the tourists. Not that you're a tourist, though,' she added kindly. 'In a month or so you'll be almost as rude about them as I am.'

Joanne returned her smile mechanically. She still felt like a tourist. This island was beautiful. She would have liked the opportunity to call it home.

From the jetty she walked around the headland until she found a sheltered cove where she could eat her lobster in privacy. She sat on the warm sand, the sun setting in soft clouds of colour over the ocean. As she settled the anger and despair of the day engulfed her. It wasn't fair!

The lobster only added to her frustrations. Eating a lobster with nothing but her fingers presented difficulties she hadn't anticipated. Finally Joanne resorted to smashing the claws between two rocks. She grimaced ruefully as she remembered the shop assistant's words. The lobster was delicious, but marred by a liberal coating of sand.

Finally she gave up. Removing her sandals, she spent an hour walking fast along the beach, her feet in six inches of water. It was hard walking and she drove herself fiercely.

Gradually the pent-up frustration within her faded and disappeared. With its disappearance came a measure of acceptance and calm. Cam's life was a tangle of unresolved emotions. She, Joanne Tynon, had enough of her own emotional scars to deal with, therefore the quicker she cut her losses and was half a world away from Cam Maddon the better.

Where to go to from here? Joanne finally allowed her weary feet to slow. She stood in the gathering dusk, gazing out to sea. There must be other beautiful places in the world. She had no ties, nothing to hold her to one place. Instead of a feeling of freedom, however, there was only bleakness.

She retraced her steps slowly, walking higher on the beach where only the occasional rush of surf swept over her feet. The moon rose, casting a silver shaft of light over the breaking waves. It was late, Joanne thought guiltily, and with the thought came the memory that no one knew where she was. It wasn't much use having two doctors on the island if one couldn't be found in an emergency. Finally she rounded the headland and made her way up the cliff to her car.

The hospital was quiet when she arrived back. The night sister smiled a greeting from the sister's station.

'You've been on the beach?' she queried, looking down at Joanne's sandy toes. 'Lucky thing. It's too good a night to be cooped up inside like yours truly.

No,' she reassured Joanne in answer to her query, 'it's been very quiet. Even old Mr Rowlands has gone to sleep without his usual fuss.'

Joanne smiled gratefully and made her way to her apartment. She flicked on her light and stopped. Seated at her kitchen table, sound asleep with his head on his arms, was Tom.

He stirred as she approached. Joanne sat down on the chair next to him and pulled him on to her lap. He looked up at her, only half awake, then nuzzled sleepily against her.

'Tom?'

'Mmm.'

'Tom, what are you doing here? You should be tucked up tight in your own bed.'

He put up a hand and clutched the soft fabric of Joanne's blouse. Joanne looked down at the little face. It was red and blotched from weeping.

'I came to tell you. . .' Through tears and sleep his voice was indistinct and Joanne had to bend to hear it. 'Don't let her take me away.'

'Tom. . .' Joanne caught her breath in horror. What did this little boy think was going to happen to him?

'She said you thought I should go to England and see another doctor. Daddy was coming too, but now he can't come yet and she's going to take me all by herself and. . .' he hiccuped on a sob '. . . I don't like her.'

Joanne bit her lip. What on earth were they doing, frightening the child like this? Tom was past being able to listen to reasoned arguments tonight, however.

'Hush,' she told him gently. 'Tomorrow I'll talk to your daddy and see if we can work something out. For now I'm going to take you back to your own bed and I'll stay with you until you go to sleep. OK?'

'OK.' A watery sniff came with his assent. His head relaxed against her and before she had carried him halfway across the lawn he was asleep.

Joanne entered Cam's flat to find a nurse emerging from Tom's empty bedroom. She greeted Joanne and her precious bundle with relief.

'Oh, thank heaven for that! It was so quiet on the wards I spent longer than usual over supper, and it's been three quarters of an hour since I checked him. I nearly died when I realised he was missing.'

'Where's his father?' Joanne asked grimly.

'Need you ask?' The girl raised her hands expressively. 'Over at the Coral Sands with that woman again.'

Joanne smiled bleakly to herself. Lindy was not making herself liked on the island. She shook her head as the girl in front of her reached out for Tom.

'No, I'll put him to bed. You needn't bother checking him either. I'll stay with him until his father gets home.'

It was two hours later before a firm tread in the corridor signalled Cam's return. Joanne stirred stiffly in the chair beside Tom's bed. She had been glad she had stayed. Tom's sleep was still troubled. Every now and then he would mutter in his sleep and half wake. Each time, Joanne's soft voice settled him again.

Cam's stride stopped abruptly at the sight of Joanne emerging from his son's bedroom.

'Joanne,' he said blankly. Then, in swift concern, 'Is something wrong?'

Joanne shook her head. 'Nothing that can't be cured by two parents acting like parents,' she said bitterly.

'And what's that supposed to mean?'

'I mean, how dare you tell Tom a woman he's never met until two weeks ago is going to take him away from everything he knows and loves, and then calmly leave him with a night nurse checking him every half-hour? It's enough to give a much older child than Tom nightmares.'

'Is that what happened?'

'He came to find me,' Joanne said steadily. 'He sees me working with Lindy to pack him off to England.'

'Well, you did say he was fit to go,' Cam said mildly.

Joanne drew in her breath. 'Cam, just because I won't tell lies I'm not going to be held responsible for the hurt you and Lindy are inflicting on your son. I won't sign a certificate saying Tom is unfit to travel, any more than I'll sign a certificate saying he needs urgent medical attention. So you can stop playing your silly little games and concentrate on the only thing that matters, and that is that you've got a very upset and disturbed little boy.'

Cam stared at her in silence, then crossed to the sideboard. He poured himself a finger of whisky and downed it at a gulp.

'Hell.'

'It is, isn't it?' Joanne agreed mildly. Then, as the silence stretched out, her curiosity got the better of her. 'Why is Tom now leaving with his mother? I thought you were all going.'

'We were,' Cam said grimly. 'Only your resignation has prevented that. Of course I can't leave the hospital unattended, whatever your scruples on the subject may be.' Joanne gasped at the injustice of the remark, but he continued inexorably, 'I have to wait for new doctors to be appointed.'

'Well?'

'Lindy won't wait that long,' Cam said patiently. 'I've agreed to let her take Tom as soon as his passport comes through and I'll come when I can.'

'She knows you'll come, then,' Joanne said softly.

'That's not the issue. Lindy wants her son.'

'Does she?'

Cam's eyes narrowed in irritation. 'Of course she does. Why else would she be here?'

Joanne bit her lip. She didn't like this, but she was determined to say something. Tom was her patient now anyway; she had the right to speak up on his behalf.

'Cam, I don't know,' she said softly. 'All I know is that Tom doesn't like her. Perhaps,' she said placatingly as his brow furrowed, 'he doesn't really know her.'

'Well, why do you think I've been taking him over to the hotel so often? It's Lindy's only chance to get to know him. I only went myself tonight because there were travel arrangements Lindy wanted formalised and Tom kicked up a fuss.'

'Lindy doesn't need you around in order to form a relationship with Tom,' Joanne replied firmly. 'Tom's finished school at three in the afternoon and has all the weekend free. Why doesn't Lindy take him off to the beach by herself?'

'She doesn't drive,' Cam said shortly.

'Well, if she's staying at the Coral Sands she's hardly short of a taxi fare,' Joanne retorted, grimacing to herself as she heard the edge back in her voice.

They stood glaring at each other. Joanne met his eyes squarely. What she was arguing for was important. In the bedroom behind them, Tom stirred and muttered in his sleep.

Cam walked past her into the darkened room beyond, and Joanne heard his low reassurance to his son. A dull ache was stirring within her. What was she doing? Fighting to make it easier for Lindy to reclaim her son? All she knew was that she couldn't wave goodbye to Tom without having made some effort to help him. She stood and waited.

By the time Cam reappeared she knew what she had to do. Cam had said her decision to resign now, forcing Cam to stay on the island, was petty. He was right. She had done it to punish Cam and Lindy. Now she saw that the person who was going to be most hurt was Cam's little son.

'You can go,' she told him quickly, before her resolution wavered.

'What do you mean?' He pulled the door gently closed behind him and turned to look at Joanne.

'I'll stay.' She closed her eyes. 'I'm not going to be the cause of hurting Tom any more than he has to be. Get his passport and go back to England. I'll stay and attempt to look after things until the new doctors come.'

'Despite my having asked for your resignation?' Cam was looking at her curiously.

She laughed, a bitter, discordant note echoing in the room. 'Look, let's leave that, shall we? You've decided I'm not suitable for the island and I accept that. You also want me to stay until the board can find replacements. Well, I accept that too. You never know, with you gone the hospital board might be more inclined to accept me as a permanent doctor. At least I'd have a chance to prove myself without being judged by your prejudiced criteria. Anyway, that's beside the point.

At the moment I'm agreeing to your requests. I only want one thing from you in return.'

'Which is?'

'That you use the fortnight or so before Tom's passport comes through to reassure Tom that his mother likes him. Leave her with him. Let him see how much she wants him for himself, not how much she wants him for you.'

'Joanne, that's an unfair comment.'

'Is it? Well, if it is then I can bear to be proved wrong. You've got a little boy who is scared stiff of his mother. Fix it.' She gave him one last glare and stalked out.

'Joanne. . .'

Joanne didn't respond. As she retreated, running light-footed back across the lawn, she sensed his eyes following her until she reached the sanctuary of her apartment.

The night was humid and oppressive. Joanne slept badly, and when she did sleep she was troubled by twisted dreams. She woke to find her pillow wet and realised that she'd been weeping in her sleep.

She had to swim. Her head ached with the dull throb of a bad night's sleep. If she was going to get any work done today somehow she had to clear the fog that was engulfing her. She was exhausted and emotionally torn, but the sea was calling.

She had barely hit the water when Cam appeared.

As soon as she saw him she stopped her rhythmic swim and turned in to the shore. It was physically impossible for her to keep swimming with the thought of him watching her. With Cam here the sea was no longer a sanctuary, and she just wanted to grab her sarong and make her escape. The throb in her head worsened. Why couldn't he leave her alone? Surely he could see the effect he had on her.

He met her at the water's edge. Joanne would have brushed past him, but he strode towards her and blocked her path. Clad only in his bathers, his muscled body dwarfed hers. She was aware that as long as he chose to keep her here there was nothing she could do to prevent it.

'Let me go,' she said icily as he grasped her shoulders to prevent her passing.

'Joanne, we need to talk.'

'We talked of everything we needed to last night. What on earth is there left to say?'

He retained his hold. 'Joanne, did you sleep as badly as I did?'

'I've got no idea. What possible interest is it to you how I slept?'

'Just that I think I love you.'

Joanne gaped up at him. Her mouth must have dropped in amazement, for he gave a sardonic grimace.

'Crazy, isn't it?' His expression, when she met his look, was devoid of anger and hostility. There was the trace of pain she had seen before.

'What. . .what do you mean?'

His mouth twisted into a bitter grimace. 'As I said, I couldn't sleep last night. I'd spent a couple of grim hours with Lindy, haggling over Tom's future, still at one level believing I was emotionally involved with her. Then I came back to the flat, and there you were, caring for my son, putting yourself second in your concern for him.'

'Is that why you say you love me?' Joanne's voice was a tiny whisper, laced with pain.

'No.' The word was jerked out of him, and she looked up, the beginning of wonder stirring in the back of her mind. 'I think I've known it for a long time. I think it took the stupid comparison of last night to see it. You're everything Lindy isn't.'

Joanne's heart twisted. 'I don't think that's a good reason to love someone.'

'No?' He smiled gently down at her. 'How about my realising that, if anything happened to you, I don't think I could cope? That to calmly leave this island and leave you to the attentions of William Langdon would tear me apart? That I don't think I can live without you? Is that crazy?'

'N. . .no.'

'Not crazy?'

She looked up at him, at the deep eyes watching hers. Somewhere a knot deep inside her loosened and fell away. The anger, tension and sorrow of the last few days dissipated as if it had never been.

There was nothing else to be said. Their eyes held their own private conversation of repentance and forgiveness. They knew it, knew of each other's commitment without words being uttered.

Then they were in each other's arms, holding each other as if they could never again release the body they were holding. Warm skin against skin, their arms reached to hold, press, feel. Their faces met in a muddle of noses and lips, until they found the patience to slow, to let lips search and seek for lips.

For Joanne the world lit in a kaleidoscope of colour. The emotion she had been holding back for so long burst in a torrent of pure, shimmering joy. The love she had been feeling was returned. It was not something to be ashamed of, to be locked away as some dark, withering secret.

She found the resolution to push herself away from his body. Feeling her resistance, he released her. She backed a couple of steps from him, her eyes never leaving his face. It was there, the love she had longed for all her life. It shone from his eyes, reflecting the depths of her feeling for him. This man was her peace, her heart.

He stood watching her, sensing her need for space. His eyes were serious, only the faint creases at the side of his mouth reflecting gentle humour. Then the mouth twisted into a wry smile.

'I don't deserve you,' he said softly. 'I don't deserve your love.'

'That's a shame,' she said gently, 'because you have it. All my love.'

'After the way I've treated you. . .'

'I gave you my love before I even left Melbourne,' she told him seriously. 'The things you've been saying to me, the way you've been behaving, has only confused me. It hasn't stopped me loving you.'

Then she was in his arms, her breath being crushed as she was held in a fierce embrace. Joanne reached up and pulled Cam's face down to hers. His knees sank to allow his face to come to her level, then somehow they were both kneeling, then lying on the damp sand. Their bodies entwined, skin against skin, each glorying in the feel of the other's body against theirs. Their mouths were locked in a deep, drowning kiss that seemed as if it could never end.

It was ended by the sea. Lost to everything but their pleasure in each other, they were not conscious of the waves, increasing with the incoming tide. Suddenly their bodies were covered in a rush of foam as a curling breaker dumped its load on its unsuspecting victims.

They emerged spluttering and laughing, their kiss broken.

'We're going to drown!' Joanne choked. She pulled back from Cam's grasp. 'Let me go.'

'I've only just got you,' he grinned. 'Urk!' He kissed her eyelids in turn. 'You taste salty.'

'You can't possibly love me if you're trying to drown me,' Joanne protested.

'Wouldn't you like to end our lives together, clasped in each other's arms?' Cam demanded wickedly.

'No,' Joanne retorted with asperity, then ducked as another wave broke over them. 'At least, not yet. Maybe in fifty years or so.'

Cam shook his head. 'I've fallen in love with a lady with no soul. Oh, well, there's only one thing for it.' He tightened his clasp around Joanne's waist. Before she knew what he was about she was being rolled up the slope of the beach, first under Cam as he carefully protected her from his weight, and then raised and up over his body. Six rolls and they hit dry sand. A fine shower of grains clung and coated their wet bodies.

Joanne was weak with laughter. Her hands still clung to the powerful body moving hers with such dexterity. As they ceased their roll she rubbed the grit from his back.

'You look like a rissole,' she told him lovingly. 'Nicely crumbed.'

He kissed her nose. 'I don't know what it is about you, lady,' he complained. 'You're not tasting any better.' Their mouths met and they broke away in the one recoil as each took a mouthful of sand. Joanne pushed away and was on her feet in one lithe movement.

'This lovemaking's got knobs on it,' she laughed as

she turned to run back into the surf. 'My tongue feels as if it's been sandpapered.' She hit the water and dived neatly into a wave.

For a moment Cam lay on the sun-warmed beach and watched. Joanne reached the line of deep water where the waves ceased their pounding and turned to look back at the beach. Even from that distance she could see the love still there. With a deep sense of happiness she turned back and started her rhythmic swimming.

Two lengths of the bay and he joined her, the surge of water from his powerful body announcing his presence. Joanne did not falter. There was no need.

Back and forth across the sunlit little cove, the two bodies moving in unison, Cam's more powerful stroke being held in check to keep pace with hers. They didn't touch; the wash of water from each other's body was a caress in itself.

Finally Joanne started to slow. As they neared her ledge, Cam reached out and brushed a finger against her shoulder. She knew what he was suggesting. He surged ahead and was ready to lift her out of the water, pulling her back to lie with him on the rocky shelf.

They came together. She turned into him without shyness, her arms going around to hold his cool wet body as she lifted her face to be kissed. He kissed her gently, softly, his hands reaching to draw the streaming strands of hair away from her face.

Slowly her lips started to respond, savouring the salt taste of her love. His mouth opened and her tongue moved to discover the moistness beyond. Here the taste was not of the sea. Here the taste was of Cam Maddon, the man she loved.

A fire was starting deep within her, an aching that

kept her tight against his body. She felt his body stir with his own arousal. The flimsy bathing-costumes they wore might just as well have not existed.

Cam drew back, his eyes darker than Joanne had ever seen them. They caressed her body, glorying in her flawless figure, her satin skin.

'You are magnificent,' he murmured. 'My beautiful sea maiden.'

'Complete with seaweed,' Joanne smiled shakily, removing a strand from between their bodies.

His eyes answered her smile, but his attention was elsewhere. His fingers moved to slip the straps of her costume from her shoulders, down over the gentle undulations of her breasts. His face came down intently; a taut nipple was taken between his lips to be kissed with infinite tenderness. His tongue moved, circling the tip of her breast. He moved, glancing up briefly to be reassured by Joanne's expression of rapt stillness before lowering his lips on to the other breast.

Joanne drew in her breath at the feel of him against her breast. Her body felt as if it were floating above itself, lost in an aura of exquisite pleasure. Her fingers curled themselves into Cam's damp hair, finding their own pleasure in this small possession.

Cam's mouth moved to touch the flatness of her stomach. Deep within Joanne a fire flickered and spread. An aching need screamed from within her thighs, forcing her breath to come in ragged gasps. She arched her body, groaning in pain and pleasure.

She reached to tug insistently at his arms and his mouth ceased its exploration. He looked up and their eyes met, locked in a glorious affirmation of their love. Cam lifted his body to lie full length against her. With one swift movement Joanne was lifted to lie above him, her naked breasts falling against his bare chest.

The sensation of skin against skin was almost unbearable. Joanne buried her face into a beloved shoulder and clung. Here was where she belonged. This man could do whatever he liked with her. He was hers.

'Dad!'

For a moment neither of them stirred.

'Dad!' The thin cry echoed across the bay and Joanne smiled into Cam's shoulder. Reluctantly their bodies parted.

'Whoops,' Cam grinned shakily. 'Sprung! Well,' he went on, lifting Joanne to her feet as he rose, 'perhaps it's just as well. You're not very good for my self-control.' He shaded his eyes until he could make out the tiny figure on the beach. 'What is it, Tom?' he called.

'There's been a car crash!' Tom yelled back importantly. 'The ambulance has just gone. Matron said to come and get you.'

Cam grimaced. 'Well, there's an end to a lovely interlude.' He gave Joanne a quizzical look. 'Can we continue this discussion at some later date?'

'Yes, please, Cam,' Joanne replied unsteadily, and he bent to give her a brief, hard kiss on the mouth.

'I'll go. You take your time.' His body dived flawlessly into the water, hardly raising a splash.

Joanne watched as he coursed his way through the blue-green water. Tom met him at the water's edge. He was lifted in a bear-hug and his squeal of delight at having his clothes soaked echoed across the bay. He was released, a small hand taken in a large one, and father and son disappeared.

Joanne was left to make her way back to the hospital

herself. She also didn't waste time. Most accidents on the island were minor; the roads didn't lend themselves to accidents involving speed, but there was a chance she could be required.

Fifteen minutes later she entered Casualty—and recoiled in horror. This was no minor accident.

The room reeked of alcohol. On a trolley near the doorway a young man, soaked in blood but fully conscious, let off a steady stream of invective. Two other trolleys had been drawn further into the room. Surrounded by the hospital staff, the figures on these trolleys appeared to be still.

Before she could move into the room, Joanne's arm was clutched by the youth on the trolley by the door.

'For God's sake, will you do something?' he moaned. 'I've broken me arm and no one will come near me. How long do I have to lie here before I get attention?' His voice rose to an angry, slurred yell, and Joanne realised where the smell of alcohol was coming from. One of the ambulancemen broke away from the group at the centre of the room and came towards her.

'Leave him, Doc,' he said harshly. 'Doc Maddon's had a look. He's got a fractured arm, but you can't do much until the effects of the alcohol have worn off. Morphine with what he's already got on board could do anything.'

Joanne glanced at the figure clutching her arm. When she looked closely she could see that most of the blood came from a superficial cut on his forehead. She nodded.

'What happened?'

'This idiot,' the officer eyed the figure on the trolley beneath them, 'is as drunk as a wheelbarrow. He's been drinking all night, went to sleep for an hour or so and decided he was sober enough to drive down to the cove for a swim. If he'd managed to get there, he probably would have drowned himself.' He looked down in disgust. 'It might have been better for all concerned if he had. Oh, for heaven's sake!' This as the youth started tossing from one side of the trolley to the other, moaning theatrically, with the odd four-letter invective at his lack of immediate attention thrown in. 'He came around the bay road on the wrong side. Young Christy Williamson and her little girl were unlucky enough to be coming the other way.'

While they were talking, Joanne had disengaged the young man's clutching hand and was walking towards the other two trolleys. Cam's attention was fully taken up with the mother, but one look at the little girl was enough to tell Joanne that here was where the immediate need lay.

Cam looked briefly up at her. 'There's not a lot for us to do here,' he said briefly. 'Christy's got severe head injuries and by the look of the little girl I think she may well lose her left foot. We've called for the air ambulance from Cairns. All we can do is try and stabilise them so they'll make it there.'

For the next couple of hours no one in the Strathleath hospital had time to draw breath. The injuries of the mother and little girl were horrific. The plane arrived, but the mother's condition was too critical for her to be moved. Finally Cam and Joanne took her to theatre to establish an airway by insertion of a tracheostomy tube before they were able to move her.

As soon as she had finished giving the anaesthetic, Joanne left Cam to finish up in theatre and made her way back to the little girl's bedside. The yelling of the wounded youth was still echoing through the hospital, but he had been moved into a private cubicle. At least Joanne didn't have to look at him.

A group of burly men were waiting in the room outside the theatre, fishermen by their appearance. One of them broke away from the group and came towards her.

'I'm Ted Williamson.' His hand reached out to clasp hers, more in anxiety than greeting. 'My wife and kid are here. Are they. . .?' He broke off, averting his face.

'They're alive,' Joanne said gently. 'Your wife's in theatre at the moment. She's got multiple fractures to her face and we've had to operate so she can breathe.'

'Oh, my God,' he whispered. 'Christy. . .'

'We're going to fly them both to Cairns within the next hour,' Joanne continued, gripping the big man's hands in hers. 'They both need urgent specialist attention. The type of surgery they need requires the facilities of a major hospital.'

'They're. . .they're going to make it?'

'I don't know yet,' Joanne had to say. It was cruel to give false reassurance. 'Your wife is critically ill. We have no way of assessing the severity of the head injuries yet. It's going to be a while before we know.'

'And Laura?'

Joanne met the man's look, her eyes not flinching from the raw pain she saw there.

'Laura has lost a huge amount of blood. She's got very bad lacerations which are going to require a skilled plastic surgeon to stitch. What we're worried most about with Laura is her leg. It's been crushed, and she may well lose it. Once again, it's too early to say, but the faster we get them to Cairns the better. Mr Maddon will be going with them. Will you go too?'

'Yes. . . Yes!'

'Have you got someone who could go with you?' Joanne asked gently. 'You're going to need a bit of support.' She looked towards the group of men who had accompanied him. One of them came forward.

'I'm Ted's brother, Doc. I'll go with them.' He cast a worried look up at his brother.

'Good.' Joanne glanced at her watch. 'Look, both Laura and Christy are still unconscious. We'll have them at the plane in twenty minutes. Have you got time to go and grab some things so you can stay in Cairns for a few days? A couple of shirts for you and, if you can, a few things to help Laura. A couple of favourite toys, a special blanket if she has one.'

The men nodded.

'Good. Be at the airport in twenty minutes. Don't break any speed limits—the plane will wait for you.' She turned to the brother. 'Don't let Ted drive. And take it easy yourself.' It had happened before that someone had been so churned up by the news of an accident that they had caused another one.

She left them and went swiftly down the corridor to Laura. She was deeply asleep. Sedation at this stage was important to alleviate the shock. Joanne checked her. Her breathing was becoming deeper. Joanne closed her eyes in thankfulness. At least this little girl seemed as if she would live. If only they could say the same for her mother.

She checked the foot again and winced. There was nothing she could do. If Laura was to keep it there would be months of reconstructive surgery ahead of her.

She stayed with the little girl until the ambulance officers came to wheel the trolley out for the trip to the airport. Joanne followed, reluctant to see the last of the child. Cam was already in the ambulance, beside the still form of Christy Williamson.

'I'll be back tonight or tomorrow,' he said briefly, his eyes not leaving Christy's face. 'Could you talk to Tom when he gets home from school? I don't like to be away tonight. He's upset enough as it is, but I haven't a choice.'

Joanne nodded. She couldn't go in his place. Christy and Laura needed the best care possible and, as the more experienced doctor, only Cam could provide it. The doors swung shut and the ambulance made its way out of the hospital grounds.

As she walked back into the hospital Joanne nearly collided with one of the junior nurses. She reached out to steady the girl and realised that the nurse's eyes were red with weeping.

'Hey, what's wrong?'

'It's that. . .that animal in there.' She caught herself and ran a hand across her eyes. 'I'm sorry—Christy Williamson is a friend of mine.' The girl gestured behind her to the casualty cubicle where the drunken driver was still yelling obesenities. 'He called me a. . . Well, it doesn't matter what he called me. When I told him both doctors were busy with Christy and Laura he told me they could die for all he cared, but he wanted some attention, now.'

'Well.' Joanne took a deep breath. She placed a hand firmly on the girl's shoulder. 'Come on, then.' She sighed. 'I guess we'd better give him some.'

CHAPTER TEN

CAM returned to the hospital late that night. Joanne had spent a frantic day trying to catch up on the normal work of two doctors. Periodically she had been called away from her surgery to attend to the demands of the young driver, his arm now set. Joanne would have liked to send him home, but his bump on the head, plus his still semi-inebriated state, really meant that he should be under observation for twenty-four hours. By the time she got rid of him it was going to feel like ninety! His alcoholic state meant that she had to go lightly with the painkillers, and every time a twinge of pain broke through he turned into a spoiled three-year-old. Worse, Joanne thought ruefully. Any three-year-old throwing the invective of her drunken patient would have had his mouth washed out with soap long since. She longed to do just that.

She had retired, exhausted, to her flat half an hour ago, only to be called back by a distracted night sister.

'My arm's hurting!' the young man threw at Joanne as she walked into the ward.

Joanne sighed and picked up his chart. He'd had a painkiller an hour ago. It was a simple fracture; the pain should not be breaking through very much.

'Mr Lohrey, I can't give you any more drugs. You've been badly bruised. I'm afraid you'll just have to tolerate a little discomfort.'

'Discomfort!' he hissed. 'I'm in bloody agony! Do I have to be dying to get any attention around here? I bet you don't tell Christy Williamson and that brat of a kid of hers that they can't have more drugs.' He laughed as he saw Joanne flinch. 'Struck home there, didn't I? Now,' his voice raised to a yell, 'get me some more bloody dope!'

Joanne closed her eyes and forced herself to do a slow count. When she opened them she was under control again.

'I'm sorry, Mr Lohrey, I can't do that. If you stop throwing yourself about and lie still you'll find the pain will ease.'

'Well, if you won't give it to me, get me someone who will,' he demanded. 'You're not the senior doctor here, anyway. Where's the boyfriend?'

'Did you want me?' Cam appeared at the door. Joanne's eyes flew to his face. His expression was one of exhausted defeat.

'Get me some bloody dope,' the man on the bed demanded. 'This little pretence at a doctor here thinks I can survive on aspirin every four hours.'

'You amaze me,' Cam responded quietly. 'Dr Tynon, I think we could cut Mr Lohrey back to medication every six hours.'

Joanne smiled grimly but shook her head.

'No? Very well, I leave him in your capable hands. If he were in mine I'd have discharged him hours ago.' He made to leave, but then turned back to the bed. 'Mr Lohrey, I don't know whether you're at all interested, but Christy Williamson died this afternoon.'

Joanne nodded. The extent of the girl's injuries and the look on Cam's face as he had entered had made her expect it. She looked down at the youth on the bed. There was no reaction.

'So what's that to me?'

Cam was quiet for a moment and Joanne sensed that he also was fighting for calm.

'Well, for one thing, it just might mean that you'll be facing a charge of manslaughter. I came back on the police launch from Cairns. They're waiting to interview you as soon as Dr Tynon is finished.' He turned and walked out of the room, not waiting to observe the interesting effect his words had on Joanne's patient.

Ten minutes later Joanne returned to her flat to find Cam there, in much the same position she had found his son previously, his head buried in his arms at ther table. She left him be while she made coffee, casting covert glances at him while she did so. Finally she laid a steaming mug in front of him, then sat and drank hers.

Finally he raised his head. His face was haggard, etched with weariness and anger.

'I have never come so close to hitting a patient,' he said softly.

Joanne nodded but said nothing. There was nothing that could be said.

'He'll go to gaol for six months and think he's been really hard done by. And Laura Williamson is going to have to get by for the rest of her life with no mother and one foot shorter than the other.'

'They've saved the foot?' Joanne asked quickly, desperate for some good news.

'I think so. I've been in theatre assisting Cairns' orthopaedic and vascular surgeons all afternoon. The police were waiting to see me when I came out of theatre, so I hitched a lift back to the island in their launch.' He ran a hand wearily through his hair. 'Is Tom asleep?'

The assumption that Joanne would have cared

enough to check was implicit in the question. She nodded.

'I had a long talk to him when he got home from school. I also had Matron ring Lindy and explain why you wouldn't be over tonight. She suggested Lindy might like to have Tom on his own, but I don't think the suggestion found favour.' She kept her voice carefully neutral, and Cam nodded.

'Thanks.'

'Drink your coffee.'

Joanne set down her empty mug, rose and went to stand behind him. As he slowly drank, cradling the cup as if drawing comfort from the warmth, she laid her hands on his shoulders and gently massaged. The tension she could feel in him slowly eased. His head came back and rested heavily against her breast.

'Nice.' He sounded almost asleep.

Joanne smiled. 'You've earned it. You don't get many days worse than today.'

'Joanne?'

'Mmm?'

'Will you sleep with me tonight?'

She turned it over in her mind. 'You mean, sleep?'

The smile returned to his voice and he turned to pull her down on to his knee. 'No, my love, I don't mean sleep.'

'That's what I thought.'

'Too soon?'

'Are you sure you love me?' she asked softly.

'I love you, my golden girl.'

'And have you got the wherewithal to stop us making babies?'

He groaned. 'Oh, the practical mind.'

'Well, someone's got to be,' she said primly.

He kissed her on the white skin of her throat. 'I have the wherewithal to stop us making babies,' he agreed gravely.

'Then it's not too soon.'

He met her eyes then with a long, serious look. 'Are you sure, my heart?'

'I'm sure.'

'But it's your first time.'

She laughed. 'Cam Maddon, I hadn't even been kissed before I met you. You are my first and only love.'

'And you'll give yourself to me?'

'With all my heart.'

After that there was no need for words. Cam lifted her and carried her gently into the bedroom. The intensity of the morning's lovemaking had gone; there was only a quiet sureness of each other.

Within moments their clothes had been discarded. They had not bothered with the light; the soft moonbeams flickering through the shades were enough for what they needed to see.

At the back of her mind, Joanne marvelled at her lack of shyness, at her readiness for what seemed so right.

Then the thought was driven from her mind as she was gathered into the arms of the man she loved and they dropped to lie on the cool linen. His body against hers was all that mattered. There and then they became one. Their bodies merged in a glory of love and they were bound together as surely as any wedding vows could ever tie them.

Afterwards they lay, sated and sleepy, yet not wanting the oblivion of sleep to overcome them.

'I'm going to have to go,' Cam said reluctantly. 'The staff stop checking Tom after I get home. I don't want him to wake and go looking for someone.'

'We'd be discovered then, for sure,' Joanne agreed sleepily. 'Oh, Cam, no one ever told me it would be this good.'

'Perhaps no one's ever had it this good.' Joanne couldn't see his expression, but she could hear his smile in the dark. His arm tightened around her shoulders and she snuggled her head into his shoulder.

'Will you mind living in England?' he asked suddenly, and Joanne's brow creased.

'In England?'

'I'm still going to have to go to England,' Cam said gently. 'I can't see Lindy relinquishing her claim on Tom just because I'm marrying you.'

'Are you marrying me?'

'Didn't I tell you that?' He ran a hand lazily down her body, from the hollow of her throat, down through her breasts, across the flatness of her belly and into the moist crevice below. 'I must have forgotten.'

'You're supposed to make extravagant promises before you make love,' she reminded him, her nerves tingling with pleasure from his touch. 'You've had your wicked way now. What use is a promise?'

'Haven't you ever heard of testing a product before purchase?' he grinned. 'Ouch!' He lifted his hand to stop Joanne's pummelling fist.

'Will you still go as soon as Tom's passport comes through?' Joanne asked wistfully as he pulled himself up to sit on the side of the bed and started to re-dress.

'I think I have to,' he said gravely. 'I know I could delay it, but Lindy would make a fuss, both legal and otherwise, so I just don't see that it's worth it. As soon as you get replacements here you can join us.'

If Lindy doesn't have her way before I get there, Joanne thought sadly, her lovely bubble of joy deflating. Lindy had made Cam fall for her before. What weapons did plain Joanne Tynon have to fight the arts Lindy had at her disposal? Especially when Cam and Lindy would be together and Joanne would be half a world away.

'Why does she want you?' she asked sadly, and Cam paused in his dressing.

'I've told you before, Joanne—it's not me Lindy wants, it's Tom. She has a right to a relationship with him.'

'So why does she never want to see him when you're not around?' Joanne asked bitterly.

Cam sighed, then reached down and kissed the tip of her nose. 'You're tired, my love, and so am I. Go to sleep. We'll talk about it tomorrow.' Then he was gone.

Joanne was left to stare at the patterns made on the ceiling by the soft rays of the moon. Sleep would not come.

Tom bounded into Joanne's bedroom at dawn. He had obviously passed the stage where he felt it was necessary to knock; Joanne's bedroom was simply an extension of his territory. He clambered up on to the bed, heaving the brace heavily up over Joanne's legs.

'Are you awake?' he asked her.

'No,' Joanne lied, pulling the covers over her head. 'Go away, you incorrigible twerp! Don't you know what time it is?'

'It's six-thirty,' Tom replied virtuously. 'You should be up. Everybody else is.'

'Everybody?'

'Well,' he said consideringly, 'everybody except Dad. He told me I was a wretch and to go and annoy somebody else. I chose you.'

'Gee, thanks.' Joanne sent a silent invective to her sleeping lover.

'That's OK,' Tom replied graciously. 'I wanted to ask you two things.'

'Ask away.' Joanne hitched herself into a sitting position, adjusted the pillows behind her and pulled the little boy on to her lap. He gave a wriggle of approval and looked directly up into her face.

'You're not really going to send me back to live in England, are you?'

Joanne bit her lip. 'Tom, I'm afraid that's got nothing to do with me. The only reason I was involved was that your mother wanted me to check that you're well enough to travel. As indeed you are.' She gave him a squeeze around his middle. 'A healthier specimen than you I've yet to see. Where you live is up to your mother and your father. Nobody else.'

He looked at her consideringly. 'My mother doesn't like me.' The words came out as a statement of proven, unemotional fact.

'That's silly,' Joanne reproved, giving the little body another squeeze. 'Who could help liking you?'

'Do you?'

'Of course I do.' She dropped a quick kiss on to the top of his tousled head.

'Were you kissing Dad when I saw you on the beach yesterday?'

For a moment surprise held Joanne speechless. She stared down at the little boy blankly.

'I only wanted to know,' Tom went on reassuringly, 'because I think you and Dad should get married.'

Joanne nodded thoughtfully, her mind full of unformed responses. 'Why would that be a good idea?' she finally managed to ask.

'Well, if you married Dad then she wouldn't want us.'

Joanne forced herself to speak seriously. 'Tom, I think you've got it all wrong. Your mum wants you. She loves you and is upset that she doesn't know you better.'

'Huh!' Tom grunted. 'Does that mean you won't marry Dad?'

'It means you should make some effort to get to know your mother,' Joanne replied non-committally. 'See if you can make her your friend. It would be much easier,' she suggested, 'than shopping around for a new mother.'

'But you'll do,' Tom said decisively.

Joanne swung the little boy off her lap and set him on the floor. 'Tom Maddon, you have a perfectly good mother. You don't need two. Now I have work to do. If I don't shower now I'll be late for the rest of the day. Be off with you. Go and ring your mum up and wish her good morning.'

'I won't,' he said sullenly.

Joanne raised her eyebrows and looked at him quizzically.

'She won't even let me sit on her lap,' Tom burst out desperately. 'She says I crease her trousers.'

'And so you do,' Joanne agreed equably. 'Look— you've scrunched up my nightie.'

'You don't care about that, though,' Tom said scornfully. 'Do you?'

Joanne grinned. 'I might.' She stooped and took Tom's small hands between hers. 'Tom, if you wanted to show how grown up you were, if you wanted to make your father really happy, you'd make a big effort to let your mother be friends with you. Do you think you could try?'

He met her eyes solemnly. 'I suppose I could,' he finally agreed. 'Do you want me to?'

'Yes.' It was perhaps the hardest thing Joanne had ever said. If Lindy was to form a happy relationship with this little boy, how much more of an outsider would Joanne be? And yet, if she didn't push Tom to make the effort she would live with guilt for the rest of her life. 'She's your mum, Tom. She's the only one you've got.'

'OK.' He swallowed and met her look. 'I'll do it. Only. . .' He turned and went to the door. When he spoke again it was in a thread of a voice that Joanne had to strain to hear. 'I just wish it was you.'

Despite what she had told Tom, Joanne didn't rise as soon as he left. She lay on her back, with her hands linked under her head, and thought of a life in England. She and Cam and Tom—and Lindy.

The rest of the day was frantically busy, with both doctors working flat out to try and catch up on the backlog of work left over from the day before. In between patients Joanne turned her dilemma over and over in her mind.

The life Tom was leading here was fragmented and difficult. For all the hospital staff looked after him, Joanne recognised Tom for what he was: a lonely little boy. He needed, ached for a mother, and, like it or not, his mother was Lindy.

Whether Lindy had the ability to be a mother to him Joanne doubted, but in going back to England Cam was indicating his wish to give her a chance to try. Lindy wanted Cam back. Perhaps for Tom's sake, Joanne should give all three of them the chance to try again.

The thought went around and around in her head. At one level her heart screamed in protest at the decision she was coming to. The clear logic of her mind told her that the decision was already made. She had no choice. To stand beside Cam and encourage Tom to look elsewhere for a mother was more than she would be able to do. She had started to love the son as well as the father. The only way she could marry Cam would be if she could embrace them both, not share them both with a woman she disliked with an intensity that frightened her.

Halfway through the afternoon William Langdon appeared in the surgery to have the stitches removed from his foot. Despite her misery Joanne was still able to regard her handiwork with pride. The wound had mended beautifully.

'I should take up embroidery,' she told him proudly. 'You're a credit to me.'

'It's a shame it's not in a position that I can show off,' he agreed. 'It's going to be a bit tricky whipping my shoe and sock off at parties to display my scar.'

'Just make sure you have clean socks on when you do,' she smiled. 'It could be a great way to break up a party.' She saw him to the door.

'Don't forget our date on Saturday,' he reminded her.

'Date?'

'You're minding my hose, remember? While I dive.'

Joanne thought back to the conversation of last week and remembered the promise of a day spent out on the Reef. For a moment she hesitated, but then her resolve hardened. If she was going to do what she had to do then the less she saw of Cam in the next couple of weeks the better.

'Of course I remember,' she smiled.

Joanne broke the news of the decision to Cam late that night. She had finished her day's work, had dinner and settled down to wait. Once again, Cam had taken Tom over to spend some time with Lindy. Joanne found she could not think of the three of them together without her stomach tightening in an anguished knot. Slowly, as she sat waiting, her resolve strengthened. Finally she heard his tread on the veranda boards and a light knock signalled his arrival.

Joanne didn't rise from the chair where she had been sitting. Her heart was leaden.

Cam was halfway across the room before he sensed that something was wrong. His stride shortened and he gave her a long, hard look before stooping to drop a kiss on the top of her head.

'What is it, my love?'

'Cam, this isn't going to work.' The words were heavy, dull with loss.

'Jo. . .' Cam dropped to his knees in front of her and took her hands into his. 'What do you mean?'

'I mean I've spent today thinking and thinking. It

sounds trite, but I can't overcome it. I can't share you with Lindy.'

'No one's asking you to.'

'Yes, you are,' Joanne whispered, fighting for the right words. 'Where have you been tonight?'

'I've been with Lindy—you know that.' He looked up at her questioningly. 'Joanne, I didn't want to go tonight—I was desperate to be with you. But Tom actually asked to go.'

As Joanne had pushed him to. She winced at the irony of what she was doing, and yet a stern voice within her told her it was right.

'I know that,' she said gently. 'It's only proper that you should spend time with her. She's the mother of your son.'

'And yet I love you.'

'A fortnight ago you thought you still loved Lindy,' Joanne reminded him.

He smiled grimly. 'I hoped you'd forgotten that conversation.'

'How could I?'

'Well, I was wrong,' Cam said fiercely. 'It's true I've never really got over Lindy. When I married her I married an ideal, a fantasy of a warm, compassionate, lovely person. When she turned out to be none of those things I still ached for the memory of that belief. It's taken me a while to realise that Lindy will never change. I've been carrying around a dream, waiting for a human form to fit it. It was only when I met you that the dream and the person merged.'

Tears were slipping down Joanne's cheeks. 'Oh, Cam, don't!'

'Why not?' He pulled her down from the chair to kneel on the floor in front of him. His hand came up and stopped a sliding tear. 'I love you, Joanne. And you love me. Just because I've made a mess of my life up to now, is that going to stop us being happy? Is one mistake going to haunt us—me—for the rest of our lives?'

'Yes,' Joanne broke in desperately. 'Don't you see? Lindy hasn't let you go, and she has claims on you I can't reach.'

'Are you saying that you won't marry me?'

'Not yet,' Joanne said quietly. 'It would be wrong, and I won't do it.'

'What do you mean, "not yet"?'

'I mean if you and Tom are definitely going to England so that Tom can sort out some sort of relationship with his mother, then you don't need me on the sidelines, watching. I couldn't bear it. I'd be hoping desperately that the whole thing would fail, and if you want it to succeed it's better that I'm not there.'

'You love me though.'

'Yes,' she said desperately. She put her arms around his neck and held him to her fiercely. 'Too well to do what you're asking me to. I'm too selfish. I won't share you, knowing that Lindy is working to undermine our relationship.'

'That's nonsense.'

'Well, why else is she still calling herself Mrs Maddon?' Joanne asked wearily. 'You tell me she married again after you were divorced. She has no legal right to the name.'

'She's explained that to me. She's doing it because of Tom. She thought he'd react better to her if she used the same name as his.'

'And he'd react better to her if you and she were husband and wife.'

'Yes,' Cam agreed, his voice edged with anger, 'he would. But both Lindy and I know that that's not going to happen. How many times do I have to drum it into your head? I'm in love with you, not with that painted, silly creature who was once my wife.'

Joanne pulled back from Cam's hold and stood up. 'Cam, I know you love me. What I'm saying is that if I go to England I'm going to be torn apart as you try to re-establish Tom's relationship with his mother. Like tonight. I know I'm being stupid, but the thought of the three of you together was more than I could bear. And you're going to have to be involved whenever Tom sees his mother, aren't you?'

'Only until things settle down. At the moment Tom won't go near her without me, but that's to be expected.'

'Even though he'll approach with friendliness every staff member of the hospital?' Joanne asked incredulously.

'Joanne, you're being unfair.'

'Am I? All I know is that I believe Lindy will work very hard at resurrecting the relationship with you, as well as Tom. I don't think she's interested in one without the other.'

'But if you were my wife. . .'

Joanne thought back to her memory of the beautiful Lindy and shook her head. After at least two marriages, marriage vows were not something to be held by that lady as something to be respected and held inviolate.

'No, Cam,' she said softly. He had risen too and was standing watching her. 'I won't do it. I want to be sure in my own mind that you're free.'

'Jo, I am free.' He took her shoulders and shook her

angrily. 'I am free,' he repeated through clenched teeth.

'Then why are you going to England?'

'For heaven's sake. . .' He let her go. 'Do you want me to send Tom off to another country by himself?'

'Of course I don't.' Joanne was having trouble speaking. 'All I'm saying is that you need time to adjust to England and adjust to sharing your son. If after twelve months you're settled and happy, you've established Tom so that he can go off with Lindy on his own whenever they need to see each other and you still want me, then I'll come.' Her voice broke and the rest came out in a whisper. 'With all my heart, I'll come.'

'A year!'

'A year.'

There was silence. Cam turned away from her and went to stand at the open window. He stared sightlessly out into the dark, his fists clenched into white knuckles.

'It never ends,' he said bleakly. 'I pay, I pay and I pay. One stupid mistake. . .'

'That stupid mistake was marriage,' Joanne reminded him. 'And a child. That's what you're asking me to commit myself to. We have to be sure.'

'I am sure.' He wheeled and seized her, holding her to him with a savage strength. 'God, Jo, you're the woman I've been waiting for all my life.' He put a hand up and ran it through the waves of her hair, then down to cup her chin and force her face up so that he could look into her eyes. 'You're beautiful, sane, happy, funny. . . So much. . . Joanne, I can't wait for a year!'

'I think you must.' Joanne met his look. What she was doing was crazy, yet she knew she was right. She wanted this man without the past clinging to him, souring their future. If she lost him by taking this risk,

then she never really had him. 'You want Tom to have
a chance to learn to love his mother, this is the only
way it's possible.'

'You'll marry me in a year?'

She shook her head. 'Cam, I'm making no promises.
I won't have you bound. In a year, if you still want me,
I'll come.'

'What sort of a commitment is that?'

'It's the only commitment I'm prepared to make.'

Their eyes met. In his dark ones, Joanne read anger
as well as pain. Anger with her? She couldn't help it.
Her heart was telling her what she was doing was right.
It was her only chance at future happiness. Why was it
tearing her in two?

'You've already made a commitment,' Cam was
saying harshly. 'You're mine, Joanne Tynon. You've
given me your heart and your body.' He slid his hands
down to cup the swell of her breasts. 'You're mine.'

'I'm not.' Joanne felt the beginning of a tiny flicker
of anger. 'I can only be yours when you are free to
belong to me—and you're not. You're still entangled
with another woman, and I won't have you under those
terms.'

'You didn't think that last night.'

'Well, I should have,' she said desperately. 'I was
full of a stupid, romantic dream of living happily ever
after, and it's not going to happen. As soon as Tom
landed on my bed this morning I started looking at the
consequences of what we were doing. If you ever free
yourself from Lindy, then that's the time to make
commitments to each other. Until then, let's leave it.'

'Nothing?'

'It's got to be nothing.' Joanne's voice broke on a
sob. 'Otherwise I'm going to go mad.'

'Jo. . .'

She warded him off with her hands. 'No—please, Cam. Just go. I don't want you to come here any more.'

He stood, staring down at her in baffled fury. Joanne forced herself to meet his gaze, her look didn't falter. Inside her heart was a twisted knot of pain, but she couldn't deviate from her chosen path. Finally, very softly, he swore, then turned and left. The crash of the slammed screen door resounded through the hospital.

CHAPTER ELEVEN

AFTER a sleepless night, Joanne sought solace in her early morning swim as a means to escape the haunting demons of the night. It had worked for her before, but this morning there was no escape. Cam's eyes haunted her. They were always just beyond her, mirrored in the crystal-clear water.

Finally she gave up and swam slowly back to the shore. Tom was sitting on the sand, hugging his knees and the hard casing of his brace.

'Hi.'

'Hi.' Joanne dredged up a smile which Tom saw through at once.

'You don't look too happy.'

'I didn't have a very good night's sleep,' Joanne excused herself.

Tom turned it over in his mind and appeared to find it an acceptable excuse. 'My dad looks sad too. Did someone die in the night?'

He had to be a doctor's son, Joanne thought. What other child would jump to that conclusion?

'No, Tom. I guess we're both just a bit tired.'

'I went to visit my mum last night.'

'I know,' Joanne agreed gravely. 'Your dad said you asked to go.'

He looked at her. 'Are you pleased?'

'I think it was a very grown-up thing to do.'

He nodded. 'I think Dad was pleased too.'

'And were you nice to your mum?'

'Well,' he said honestly, 'I tried to be. It's hard, though, because she's not interested in me.'

'I'm sure that's not true.'

'It is,' he defended himself. 'She only ever wants to talk to Dad when we're there. When I interrupt she looks at me.'

'Looks at you?'

'Yeah,' he agreed. 'Like I'm a pest.'

Joanne had retrieved her sandals and sarong. Now she took a small hand in hers and they started off down the path. A germ of an idea was starting up in her head.

'Tom, if your mum doesn't have time to talk to you when your dad is there, perhaps you should ask if she'll take you off on your own some time.'

'Just her and me?'

'Just you and your mum,' Joanne agreed.

'She wouldn't like that,' Tom said decisively.

'How do you know if you've never tried it? Besides, it must get pretty boring on your own around the hospital when your dad's on duty. Why don't you ask if she'll take you to the beach, or on a picnic or something?'

He turned it over in his mind. 'I might,' he agreed reluctantly.

'Think it over,' Joanne agreed. 'I'll tell you what— on Saturday I've been invited out for the day, so your dad will be on duty. Why don't you talk to your mum about having you for the day?'

'A whole day with her?' Tom's voice rose in incredulity.

'You never know,' Joanne smiled. 'You just might have fun.'

* * *

Joanne spent most of that next twenty-four hours avoiding Cam. She performed her work mechanically, working in a haze of misery. If she walked into a ward and Cam was there she made an excuse to leave and come back later. During clinic she even found herself trying to time patients so she called another in when Cam was safely in mid-consultation.

Finally it was night, and she mentally crossed a day off her list of fourteen that would have to be endured before he left. And after that?

It would be so easy to agree to go. Cam wanted her, she told herself. She could be near him, even be married to him. And then the image of Lindy rose up, always living near, always being able to call on Cam to spend time with her. It was impossible, Joanne thought bleakly, to build their relationship under those conditions. If Cam couldn't see it then she was going to have to make the decision for both of them.

The mood of the hospital was sombre. Cam had imparted his decision to Matron, who had informed the rest of the staff. When Joanne came into the hospital kitchen on Friday evening, Mrs Robb was unashamedly weeping.

'I can't help it,' she apologised to the rest of the staff. 'I'm going to miss that little boy so much.' She sniffed. 'He's got to feel almost like one of my own. Oh, lord, now I've burnt the steak!'

It didn't matter. None of the staff seemed particularly hungry. Having made token efforts to eat they dispersed back to the wards, their usual cheerful gossip sadly quiet.

By the time Saturday dawned Joanne was aching to get out of the confines of the hospital. She had to let

Cam know where she was going, though. It took an almost herculean effort to knock on his door.

'I knew you were going out for the day,' Cam said brusquely after she had explained the reason for her presence. 'Tom told me.'

'Is he going out with his mother?' Joanne asked eagerly, and Cam gave her a strange look.

'Yes. He asked her last night if he could spend today with her. Lindy has some reservations, but I'm dropping him at the hotel at ten o'clock.'

I'll bet she had some reservations! Joanne thought savagely, but out loud she simply said quietly, 'I'm meeting William at the hotel around about then. Why don't I drop him off?'

'You're spending the day with William Langdon?' Cam's voice was tight and controlled.

'He's taking me out to the reef in his boat. We're taking a picnic lunch. William said to tell you he has a radio on board if I'm needed urgently.'

'That's considerate of him.'

'He's a considerate man,' Joanne said quietly. 'A friend.'

'Fine,' Cam said shortly. 'I'll send Tom over to your flat at nine-thirty. Have an enjoyable day with your "friend".'

They stared at each other for a long moment, the hurt in Joanne's eyes met with anger in Cam's. Finally Joanne turned away and retreated, her eyes blinded by unshed tears.

Tom was quiet as well. He climbed into Joanne's little car and sat with his hands folded, staring straight ahead during the drive across the island.

'What do you think you'll do today?' Joanne asked gently.

'I don't know.' Tom looked down at his hands. 'I don't care really.'

'Did you bring your bathers?'

'They're in my bag.' His voice held a complete lack of interest.

'Well. . .' Joanne reached over and ruffled a small head. 'A day at the beach couldn't be all bad, could it?'

Tom's expression said that it could. He resumed staring straight in front of him. Daniel, off to be fed to the lions, Joanne thought grimly.

She took Tom up to Lindy's room before she went to find William. Tom knew the way but had to be prodded to lead her. Finally he indicated a door, and Joanne knocked.

'Cam! Darling, you're early.' A laughingly reproachful voice sounded from within, and the door swung open to reveal Lindy with nothing except a scanty towel hiding her naked loveliness. Tom backed into Joanne's legs as Lindy's expression changed from welcome to distaste.

'You!'

With an effort, Joanne dredged up a smile. 'Here's Tom, Mrs Maddon.'

'Where's Cam?'

'He's still at the hospital. I was coming this way, so I offered to bring Tom over.'

'How kind.' The woman's voice was like a douche of cold water. She held out a hand imperatively to Tom, who backed tighter into Joanne. 'Come on.' Already there was irritation.

Joanne stooped and gave the little boy a quick hug.

'Off you go and enjoy yourself,' she said firmly. 'Tell me all about it tonight, OK?'

'OK.' He gave a watery sniff and let her go. Taking a deep breath, he walked into Lindy's room and the door was slammed shut. Joanne was left feeling as if she personally had just fed him to the lions.

Out on the bay with William, Joanne fought to forget the emotion of the last few days. The sun was shining, the sea was sparkling and William was exerting himself to be good company. Despite her misery he finally made her laugh.

'That's better,' he said approvingly. 'It's the first proper grin I've seen all morning.'

'I'm sorry,' she said ruefully. 'I guess I've been caught up with my own problems. I'm being lousy company.'

'Would it help to talk?' he said sympathetically. 'Despite my propensity to bore my students to snores, I'm also a very good listener.' He moved a hand on the tiller and the little boat swung out of the bay and headed towards the open sea.

'How far do we go?'

'Only a couple of miles. Ten minutes. Now, tell Uncle William. Love-life problems?'

Joanne regarded him with indignation. 'William Langdon, this is most improper.'

'I'm right, aren't I?'

Joanne looked at him for a long moment, then finally nodded. 'Though how you guessed is beyond me.'

'Remember, I'm missing my own fiancée like crazy,' he reminded her gently. 'I guess I recognise the signs.'

In the end it was a relief to talk. The huge mass of complications resolved itself and cleared in Joanne's mind as she talked, and even before William agreed with her the remaining doubts she had been feeling had dispersed. She couldn't face sharing Cam with Lindy.

'You wait,' William said staunchly. 'He'll be back. He's mad to even go.'

'He must,' Joanne explained. 'Lindy knows him too well. She knows he's always hoped she'd love Tom and she's using it to force his hand. By not taking him back to England, she'd make Cam feel he was depriving Tom of a mother.'

'Some mother!' William snorted.

'Yes, well, you can see that and so can I, but it's something she's got enough brains to keep from Cam,' Joanne said sadly. 'She'll win in the end.' She raised her hands to her cheeks and finished in a muffled thread of a voice, 'And she'll make them so unhappy.'

'Hey, Joanne.' William stretched out a hand and took hers in a strong grip. 'I can't imagine you, Dr Joanne Tynon, Sewer of Cuts Extraordinaire, falling in love with a fool. Therefore, Cameron Maddon is not a fool and therefore all is not lost. Now, I don't know whether you've noticed, but we are now over one of the most beautiful pieces of coral reef in the world. Grab yourself a snorkel and mask and forget the mundane world above the surface for a while. Come on—this is magic!'

It *was* magic. If anything could drive the leaden oppression from Joanne's mind it was the dive that William led her on. For the rest of the morning they were lost in a world of underwater wonder.

The water around the boat varied from deep pools to ankle-depth. Standing on one of the shallower areas, Joanne felt a weird sense of isolation. No section of the reef was above the level of the water. Apart from their

solitary boat there was nothing, just miles and miles of
calm ocean surface. Joanne looked down at her feet.
They were six inches under water, clad in light canvas
shoes to protect her soles from the sharp coral, and
their possession of their coral foothold was already
being challenged by tiny, darting fish, obviously curious
about these strange intruders to their territory.

Fascinated, Joanne stooped to look more closely.
William was already submerged in one of the deeper
pools. His head broke the surface and, as he beckoned
her encouragingly, she slipped in to join him.

The kaleidoscope of colour took her breath away.
The living coral itself seemed of every imaginable shape
and hue, contorted into weird and wonderful patterns.
Weaving between the forest of coral was an infinite
variety of sea life, all of it, it seemed, intent on ignoring
these human intruders and getting on with their lives.

It was like a magnificent garden on a sunny day,
thought Joanne as she drifted lazily on the current.
Better. The best a garden could provide was bird and
butterfly life above it. Here the fish were massed in a
range of colours, shapes and sizes that defied
description.

By the time Joanne made her way back to the boat
the pain she had been carrying for the past days had
receded. It was almost as if she had been drugged, she
thought lazily, sinking her teeth into a huge slice of
watermelon William had provided. The pain was still
there, ready to resurface at the end of the day, but for
now she could at least enjoy William's company and
soak in the splendour of the reef.

After lunch William restarted the motor.

'I told you we were here to work,' he responded to
her questioning look. 'It's too good an opportunity to

miss. I need to go deep, and it's too risky without someone on the surface, making sure some twit doesn't come along and turn off my compressor.'

'As if anyone would!'

'Well, no,' William grinned. 'I doubt if anyone would be fool enough for that. All the same, it wouldn't be a particularly pleasant sensation being sixty feet below the surface and knowing that my air supply was totally vulnerable.'

'Couldn't you just come up?' Joanne asked curiously. 'If it was turned off, I mean?'

He shook his head. 'Not from that depth and with the amount of time I'll spend down there. I could come up in a hurry if I'd only been down for ten minutes or so, but if I've been down for over an hour I'd be at risk of getting the bends.'

'OK, OK.' Joanne held up her hands in acknowledgement. 'I promise I won't turn it off.'

'Good girl.' He was adjusting a blue and white flag on to a thin pole as he spoke. 'Actually this should be enough to tell anyone that there's a diver below.' He checked the coil of yellow hose and did a final inventory of his equipment. 'Now, you won't be bored?'

She smiled up at the rubber-clad figure. 'Not me. I'm perfectly content.'

He picked up her sun-hat from the bottom of the boat and placed it on her head. 'Well, keep covered—the combination of the sea and sun is murder. See you later.' He adjusted his mask and slid backwards over the side into the water.

Joanne watched him descend. The water was so clear she could make him out for quite a while, but then he disappeared among the dark shadows below. She applied another liberal coating of sun-cream and settled back against the cushions William had thoughtfully provided. The afternoon was hers.

For a while she tried to read. The effects of the sun and the aftermath of the last few days had robbed her of the ability to concentrate. If William had not been below she would have slept, but the thought of his dependence on the compressor and the snaking yellow hose floating lazily on the surface of the water kept her awake. It would have been a good time to think, make plans for the future, but her mind was still caught with the curious numbness brought on by the morning's swim. As it was, she lay back, soaking in the sunshine and gentle swell, and allowed her concentration to be caught by little things: the wheeling of a gull overhead or the investigations of the schools of tiny fish around the sides of the boat.

The roar of a motor broke into the stillness of the afternoon, and Joanne stood up and shaded her eyes. It was a large motor-cruiser, headed straight towards her.

She eyed the hose uneasily. William had said there was a hundred foot of hose in all and he wanted room to manoeuvre below the surface. The slack hose simply floated, a yellow snake waiting to be taken up.

Surely they would see the flag? As the cruiser neared Joanne started to yell, gesturing frantically towards the flag. The boat didn't even slow. As it screamed in towards her, Joanne could make out its occupants, four men all with beer cans. It veered right along the side of her little boat, tipping it crazily. They lifted their cans in a drunken salute to the pretty girl in the boat and then roared away. The yellow hose was sliced neatly in half.

Joanne stared at it. Panic rose in her, holding her

immobile. What had William said? He couldn't come up quickly.

He had no choice. But to come from sixty feet with no air?

The boat ceased its crazy sway and then jerked again as Joanne dived neatly over the side. She surfaced at the spot where the hose had been cut, searching wildly until she found what she was looking for. Here was the end that would lead her to William. Treading water, she pulled the slack hose hand over hand, desperate in her haste to reach the end.

William surfaced unconscious. His body came up face down, limp and lifeless in the water. Forcing herself to stay calm, Joanne thought back to the swimming classes at university. Under his arms, from the back. He was heavy. The swim back to the boat seemed to take forever.

Once there her problems weren't over. With one hand supporting him and the other clutching the boat there was nothing she could do. Finally she seized the hose still firmly attached to him, released his limp form and swung herself into the boat. Once in, she reached down and pulled him up so that his arms and head were over the side of the boat.

Enough. She had to stop to get some air into him. His mask was already pushed aside. Bending down at a crazy angle, all the time gripping his wetsuit to stop him sliding back into the water, she managed to check his airway and give him three deep breaths.

It wasn't going to work. Every time she tried to breathe for him he slipped backwards and she had to waste time dragging him up again.

Finally she stopped, caught her breath and took stock. She was going to have to get him into the boat.

She bent further over the back of the boat and caught him under his arms, so tightly that she could link her hands behind his back. Then she waited.

The first swell was not enough. As it lifted William's body Joanne lurched back, trying to drag him with her. The swell passed and William sank back, Joanne still clinging to him ferociously. The momentum gained by the lift and fall, however, was enough to make the back of the boat lift again. As it did a second swell caught it. Joanne jerked backwards with all her strength, and suddenly she was lying full length on the bottom of the boat with William on top of her.

Not for long. In seconds he was turned over and Joanne was breathing fiercely for him. 'Live, damn you!' she told him fiercely. 'Come on, William—live!'

In reality, the time between the hose being cut and the time William took his first spluttering breath was no more than a few minutes, but to Joanne it would live in her memory as one of the longest times of her life. No sound had ever been sweeter than that first cough. She ceased her breathing and looked up. His eyes were open.

He was conscious, but only just. His eyes reflected shock and agonising pain. As he fought for breath his hands went up and held his ears. His first sound was a long, low moan of pain.

There was little Joanne could do. She knew what would have happened. By ascending at such a rapid rate he would have burst his eardrums. She stooped to listen to his breathing. At least that was settling into a regular pattern. If he had failed to breathe out as he had risen he could have blown his lungs out. It seemed he had been spared that.

And then there was the bends—decompression sickness. After so long in the water William's body would have taken up nitrogen. Given no time to dissipate, it would now be forming bubbles. Without fast access to a decompression chamber, William was looking at paralysis or even death through an embolism or brain haemorrhage. Already he was drawing his knees up, trying to alleviate the pain caused by bubbles of nitrogen on his joints.

Joanne pushed the cushions behind William's head and stood up. He was moaning softly, lost in a haze of shock and pain. She was on her own.

There was a radio. Heaven knew how to work it, but she had to try. Tentatively she turned it on. There was a dial, with 'Emergency' marked in red against one position. With this in position she picked up the handset.

'This is an emergency. Can anyone hear me?'

Nothing.

She looked down at the handset, willing it to work. On the handset itself was a button. Holding it down, she tried again.

'Please, this is an emergency. Can anyone hear me?'

Silence, then magically the silence was broken. 'Police and emergency services here.' It was a male voice. 'What's the problem?'

Joanne took a deep breath and again pushed down the 'send' button.

'It's Dr Joanne Tynon here. I'm in a small boat out from Strathleath Island. My companion has just had his hose cut while diving. He. . .' She looked down at William's contorted figure on the floor of the boat. 'He's urgently in need of medical attention—a decompression chamber.' She looked around her. 'I'm sorry, but I don't even know really where I am. I think we're about two miles out, north of the island.'

There was a silence from the other end, for so long that Joanne started to react with panic. Then the crackling voice resumed.

'Dr Tynon, you said?'

'That's right.'

'And you're out there with William Langdon?'

'Yes.' Joanne reacted with surprise.

'He usually lets us know when he's diving and this morning he mentioned that you'd be with him,' the voice reassured her. 'Dr Tynon, do you know anything about boats?'

'This is the first one I've been in,' Joanne stated, her voice steadier than she felt.

'That's OK.' The voice was measured and reassuring. 'With the reefs around here you need to know the area before you get any speed up, otherwise you'll end up holing the boat. Look, just sit tight, leave the radio on and I'll find out who else is in the area.'

The voice ceased. Joanne used the time to crouch beside William. Gently she told him what was happening. She wasn't sure whether he could hear; with burst eardrums it was unlikely. Occasionally his pain-filled eyes met hers, only to fall away as he was consumed with another agonising spasm. She dipped a towel in sea-water and bathed his face. He couldn't take much more of this.

The crackle of the radio announced the return of the voice. Joanne grabbed the handset in relief.

'Dr Tynon?'

'Yes.'

'There's a fishing-boat just north of you. I've directed them to the reef. They're going to have to work their

way along the reef to find you. If you can, put
something bright at the top of your flag.'

Joanne's beach towel was a splash of crimson and
yellow. Within moments it was hoisted high, tied on by
the smaller blue diving-flag.

'OK,' the voice resumed. 'As soon as they reach you
they'll take you on board. They're a big vessel, so they
should   have   emergency   medical   supplies.   I've
instructed them to bring you straight to the mainland.'

'Not back to Strathleath?'

'It would waste time—the decompression chamber's
in Cairns. This way will be fastest.'

Joanne accepted his decision without argument. She
had never felt so helpless in her life.

It wasn't more than ten minutes before she spotted
the fishing-boat. It was large and travelling fast. As it
sighted her it slowed and swung in to come alongside.
The men were competent and efficient; in moments
both she and William were aboard the bigger vessel
and were on their way to Cairns, their little boat
bobbing madly in their wake.

Their drug cupboard, wonder of wonders, produced
morphine.

'We often stay out for weeks on end,' one of the
fishermen told Joanne. 'We get special permission to
carry it. One of the boys had to go and do a course to
learn to give an injection if he ever needed to. Still,' he
added reflectively, 'he's not going to be too cut up that
you're here to give it. We've been thinking he was a
bad choice to have the training ever since we heard he
passed out when his missus had the last baby.'

Joanne smiled perfunctorily, her mind occupied with
what she was doing. Finally the morphine was administered and the dreadful pain eased from William's
eyes. He drifted into an uneasy sleep.

'Eh, he looks bad,' he companion murmured as he helped her wrap the sleeping form in thick woollen blankets. Joanne could only agree.

By the time they reached Cairns shock was starting to take its toll on Joanne. One of the fishermen had found her a thick woollen guernsey which she pulled on over her bikini and T-shirt, but despite its warmth her teeth were still chattering. An ambulance was waiting at the wharf. Sitting in the back as it screamed its way to hospital, she looked ruefully down at herself. She hardly presented a professional appearance.

For the first time she noticed traces of blood on her thigh and examined with interest a massive bruise, caused no doubt by that desperate lunge backwards into the boat. She guessed it would hurt later. For the moment she was past caring. She wished William would regain a little colour. She leaned forward and listened to his breathing. It was still steady.

Then they were at the hospital and the awful responsibility was ended. There was a competent medical team for whom the treatment of decompression illness was standard. They greeted Joanne with courtesy and kindness, but her role as doctor was over.

William was placed immediately into a decompression chamber, and the doctor in charge went in with him.

'He'll stay in here for about five hours now,' he explained to Joanne. 'I'll stay with him for the first couple of hours. If you like you could take a turn on the second shift.' He eyed her sympathetically. 'Get yourself cleaned up, have a rest and see how you feel. Sister will take care of you.' He disappeared into the outer chamber, and Joanne was left with Sister, feeling very much like a dismissed relative.

A shower and a set of borrowed clothes made her feel almost human. She emerged from the nursing-home bathroom feeling almost as if she could face the world again, although, she admitted to herself, she would have preferred it if Sister Riley were a couple of sizes smaller. Beggars couldn't be choosers, though, and she folded her dubious guernsey carefully ready to be returned to the fisherman who had lent it to her.

As the strain of the afternoon eased, Joanne started to feel the physical effects of the afternoon's exertion. Her thigh was a glorious Technicolor mess and, looking backwards in the mirror after her shower, she discovered that her lower back matched. She must have landed with the full weight of herself and William on top of some nasty, unforgiving object. Her back was beginning to throb. William must weigh in at thirteen stone at least. Any physical training instructor, when asked about the advisability of lifting such a dead weight, would have told her not to be a fool.

As the warmth from the shower wore off, her body started to scream of its misuse. By the time Joanne located Sister Riley, she was limping with the pain. Sister Riley eyed her sympathetically.

'We didn't treat you as a patient when you came in. What if I get one of the doctors to give you a going over now?'

'I'll be fine,' Joanne said brusquely. 'How's William?'

'Well, that's what I've been over finding out, because I thought you'd want to know.' She beamed. 'It's a bit early to tell yet, but Dr Ross has made decompression sickness his specialty. He's seen a lot of cases and he thinks your Dr Langdon should be fine.'

'Is he conscious now?'

'He's sleeping. Once he's under the pressure of the chamber the pain eases like magic. It'll only be his ears that are causing pain, and I guess you gave him enough painkiller to cope with them.'

'And some,' Joanne agreed. 'At least his ears will get better. Sister Riley, I badly need to use a phone.'

'If it's to ring Strathleath hospital, they already know what's going on. The police on Strathleath let them know from the beginning. Mr Maddon was the one who directed the fishing-boat to come straight here. He rang himself while you were in the shower. I told him we'd give you a bed here overnight and put you on the ferry in the morning, if that's OK?'

'That's fine. There are another couple of calls I need to make, though.'

It didn't take Joanne long to get the name and phone number she was looking for. The secretary of the geology department of William's university was helpful, and moments later Joanne was talking to William's fiancée. When she finally hung up she knew that, almost as soon as William came out of his drug-induced sleep, he would have his lady beside him. She smiled a little at the thought and then grimaced at the sharp stab of jealousy knifing through her. Why couldn't she and Cam be as happy?

She made her way back to the decompression chamber and was there as Dr Ross emerged.

'Do you want to go in?' He looked closely at the strain etched on her face. 'There's no need, you know. He's sleeping so soundly he'd never know you were there. There's plenty of people here to look after him. Why don't you let Sister Riley find you some dinner and a bed? You look just about all in.'

'After you've looked at her leg, Doctor,' Sister Riley broke in grimly.

He raised questioning eyes at Joanne.

'It's only bruised.' This man had enough to do without worrying about her trivial hurt. 'Please, I'm fine.'

He looked doubtful, but Joanne was right. He was busy. She was left to be led to the hospital dining-room by a disapproving Sister Riley. She had barely finished her meal when she was called to the phone.

'Dr Tynon?'

'Yes.'

'There's a couple of men in Reception who'd like to see you.'

It was the fishermen who had brought Joanne and William in.

'We've had a good meal at the pub,' they grinned at her. 'If we stay any longer the fishing's going to get forgotten. We're heading back out now, and we wondered if you'd like a lift back to the island.'

There was nothing Joanne would like better. She wanted her own clothes, her own bed and, she achingly acknowledged, to be back near Cam.

The trip back was a balm to her tangled nerves. She stood on the deck with the big guernsey pulled on over Sister Riley's dress and soaked in the peace of the night. The sea was a black, shining mirror, reflecting the brilliant moonlight. The men seemed to sense her need for solitude. After their initial sympathetic enquiries and appreciative comments on her outfit they let her be.

Joanne's little car was still parked at the jetty, where she and William had left it. It seemed almost unreal to see it there. So much had happened since the time it had been left.

She bade goodbye to her friends with real gratitude and eased herself painfully into the car. It would be good to be home.

CHAPTER TWELVE

THE hospital was quiet as Joanne pulled into the parking bay. The evening visitors had long since gone home. Only the big light above the casualty entrance shone brightly; all the ward windows were dim.

Joanne gave a grimace as she pulled alongside Cam's car space. His car was gone. He must have gone over to collect Tom from the hotel and stayed on while the hospital was quiet, Joanne thought, trying to suppress her unhappiness. She bit her lip. She was just going to have to get used to the idea of Cam, Lindy and Tom together.

All she wanted was her bed. Climbing out of the car, she had to stop and steady herself, waiting for the shafts of pain going down her leg to ease. For a moment she considered not letting anyone know she was back. In an emergency Cam could be called from the hotel.

She couldn't do it. She could still be required for an anaesthetic. Besides, her car was now in front of the hospital, signalling her presence. She made her way through the dark garden to her flat at the back. Ten minutes later, clothed a little more respectably in her own jeans and windcheater, she emerged to find the night sister.

To her surprise, Matron Wheeler emerged from the sister's station at the sound of Joanne's approaching footsteps.

'Oh, my dear,' she said grimly. 'Oh, I'm so glad you're back.' Her normally cheerful face was creased in worry, and her voice shook. She came towards Joanne, who reached out and took her hands.

'What's wrong, Matron?'

'I. . .' The woman stopped and took a deep breath. 'It's Tom. He's missing.'

'Missing?' Joanne echoed blankly.

'Since this afternoon. He was on the beach with his mum and wandered off. They think he's somewhere in the bush, but if he's not. . .'

Joanne stared at her in horror, her mind racing. 'Since this afternoon? Is that where Cam is?'

Matron nodded. 'He's been searching from the beach at the edge of the National Park. Every available man on the island has been searching since we knew.'

Joanne was silent, absorbing this new horror. The whole thing was unreal. To be thrust from one life-threatening situation to another was too much for her tired mind to absorb. She was already deeply shocked by the events of the afternoon; now Tom's disappearance assumed nightmare qualities. Tom! She caught herself. It was going to do no good to anybody if she became hysterical. Matron was already unashamedly weeping. Joanne took a deep breath and steadied.

'All right, Matron.' She had her voice under control. 'Let's be professional about this, shall we?' She looked round to see two junior nurses sniffing dolefully at the end of the corridor. 'It seems to me that if we don't stay calm we can't expect anyone else to. Now, what needs to be done?'

Matron emerged from her handkerchief and met Joanne's eyes. There was an unmistakable message there. She swallowed and caught hold.

'I'm sorry, Doctor—I'm right now. Mr Maddon was called away this afternoon and nothing's been done since then. Luckily it's Saturday, so at least there was no surgery. There's two patients who need their drugs reviewed. I've got young Johnny Trant in Casualty who's got a building-block up his nose and Mrs Neilson's in labour. I was just about to have to call Mr Maddon from the search when you arrived.'

'Right.' Joanne assumed a cloak of efficiency, masking the sinking feeling in the pit of her stomach. 'Let's have a look at Mrs Neilson first.'

On the way down to the labour ward, out of earshot of the junior nurses, Joanne took the opportunity to ask, 'Do they have any idea where Tom might be?'

'Not as far as I know.' Matron also had assumed a brusquely efficient tone. 'Apparently he ran away. He was last seen about four this afternoon heading up the cliff into the bush.'

Joanne frowned. It didn't seem like Tom. He was a sensible little boy.

For the next hour she had to push the thought of Tom to the back of her mind. She was needed.

Mrs Neilson's baby was still a fair way off. Her labour was progressing slowly. It was a first baby. She and her husband were diligently going through the breathing techniques they had learnt during the antenatal classes, and Joanne smiled to herself as she left them to it. She sometimes wondered what people had done in labour wards before they had breathing techniques to keep them occupied.

Johnny Trant took longer. His block was firmly wedged at the back of his nose and it took Joanne considerable fiddling before she hooked it out. Luckily he was co-operative and interested. If he'd been difficult Joanne would have had to call Cam back to give a general anaesthetic. Finally the block lay in the little boy's palm.

'Gee, thanks,' he said expressively. 'It's the wheel of my Ray Buster. I would have hated to lose it.'

His mother raised her eyes heavenwards and led her young son away.

There was a ward round to be done, checking each patient's drug doses and noting changes in condition. It was necessarily short as most of the patients were asleep. It was time-consuming, however, as many of the patients were Cam's and Joanne had to read histories before making decisions. Finally Matron's needs were satisfied, and Joanne re-checked Mrs Neilson. The baby showed no signs of impending arrival, although the breathing was going beautifully.

'Would you mind if I drove over to the search and found out what was going on?' Joanne asked Matron. 'Things are quiet here for the moment. If Mrs Neilson looks like speeding up you could contact me through the police. I won't leave the search base.'

'I'd be glad if you would,' Matron agreed. 'It'd make me feel better to know what was going on.'

It was a fifteen-minute drive across to the cove where the search was based. Joanne hadn't been to that part of the island and was dismayed to realise just how densely forested the area was. The road into the cove was cut through rough, mountainous country. At least it doesn't extend far, she thought to herself. Surely they can cover the area tonight.

They couldn't. The officer in the little caravan they had towed in to act as search headquarters was grim as he showed Joanne a map. The road she had come in on crossed one of the narrowest strips of bush land. If Tom had headed in the other direction, as Lindy had told them he had, there were many miles of virgin bush. Most of it was rain forest, lush and impenetrable.

'You could pass within three feet of a kid out there and not see him,' the officer said bleakly. 'Our boys are just bashing their way through, hoping like hell to be lucky. We'll bring in extra searchers from the mainland in the morning, but there's no way we can cover all of it.'

'Where is Mrs Maddon?' Joanne asked. Try as she might, she couldn't keep the tremor of fear from her voice. 'I thought she'd be here. Is she out searching as well?'

'She. . .there was a bit of an argument with Mr Maddon,' he said shortly. 'Her friends took her back to the hotel.'

'Her friends?'

'Some people from the hotel. They arrived here on their yacht a couple of days ago, and Mrs Maddon and Tom spent the day with them.'

'Oh,' said Joanne slowly. 'I thought they were having a day alone together.'

'Not as far as I can make out,' the man went on disapprovingly. 'There's been quite a party down here—wine bottles and debris all along the beach. Mrs Maddon. . .' He looked up to assess whether he should impart such information and decided to continue, 'Mrs Maddon wasn't exactly sober.'

Joanne closed her eyes. She had as clear a picture as she wanted. The memory of Tom's pleading eyes this morning came back to her. How much was she responsible for this mess?

The sound of an approaching group of searchers brought them both to the door of the van. In the group of weary men, there was Cam. There was no need to ask if their search had been successful. It was written in the bleakness of their faces.

Cam stopped a little way short of the van. As the others grouped around the main map, marking with the search co-ordinator the area they had covered, Cam sank on to a fallen tree and buried his face in his hands. Joanne took a deep breath and approached.

'Cam?'

He looked up. In the light from the lantern beside him his face was haggard with worry.

'Jo.' There was no surprise at her presence.

She sank down to crouch on the ground in front of him, ignoring the pain in her back. Gripping his filthy hands in hers, she spoke to him urgently, trying to break through the blankness.

'Cam, he'll be found. There's no need to be pessimistic. He's only been gone for a few hours and it's a warm night. He's a sensible little boy.'

'He could have been gone since lunchtime!'

'Matron said it was four o'clock.'

'Yes, well, that was Lindy's story,' he said tightly. 'She went running to the police saying he'd run away from her. When the police questioned the rest of the people she was with, no one could remember seeing him since lunchtime. The running away story was a fabrication.'

'You mean no one checked that he was still on the beach for four hours?' Joanne couldn't keep the horror from her voice.

'That's right.' He gave a mirthless laugh. 'Some mother I provided my son with.'

Joanne turned this new information over in her head. Anything could have happened. Tom could have gone swimming. He could have. . . She gave herself a mental shake. This kind of thinking wasn't going to help Cam.

'Cam, he'll be in the bush somewhere,' she said pleadingly. 'He'll be trying to get back home. He's strong and fit. He could walk for miles.'

'He hasn't got his brace on,' Cam said shortly. Then, at Joanne's puzzled look, he continued, 'Lindy didn't want a cripple to show off to her friends. She made him take it off.'

'Oh, Cam!' Joanne sat back on her heels, soaking in the enormity of what she had been told. 'It means. . . It means he probably won't be far away,' she said tentatively.

'It means he's probably lying somewhere with a twisted ankle,' Cam said savagely. 'Or if he's tried to climb——'

'Cam, don't!'

She was holding him, rocking his rigid frame, murmuring stupid, meaningless reassurances, while all the time the tears were streaming down her face.

'Dr Tynon?' A hand touched her shoulder, and reluctantly she turned from Cam. It was the officer she had spent time with in the van. 'I'm sorry, but the hospital is on the radio. They say you're needed back there.'

Mrs Neilson. Joanne nodded. 'Tell them I'll be there in fifteen minutes.' She turned back to Cam. 'I have to go and deliver a baby. Do you. . .will you stay?'

'Do you think I'd leave?'

'No.'

There was little sleep for Joanne that night. It was three a.m. Before Mary-Ann Neilson finally arrived into the world. Joanne left the smug trio and made her way back to her flat, but there was no sleep. She lay in bed, her back an aching, throbbing pain centre. Briefly she thought of taking something to ease the pain, but she knew its severity needed something stronger than aspirin. If she was the only doctor available, she daren't take anything.

Then there was the thought of Tom. To lie on cool linen sheets seemed almost an obscenity when Tom was out there somewhere in the night. She dozed intermittently, only to wake again with the thought of Tom in her head. Finally at dawn the pain became too much to continue lying down. She rose and made her way into the hospital kitchen, where it seemed most of the night staff were sitting staring morosely at cups of cold coffee. At the sight of her, they disappeared back to their various tasks, but Joanne knew there was going to be very little efficiency in the hospital until Tom was found.

Halfway through the morning she drove over to search headquarters again. It was a hive of activity. There was no sign of the searchers—they were dispersed in groups throughout the bush—but the ladies' auxiliary had arrived in force. Momentarily deprived of the objects of their mercies as they were, Joanne found she was regarded as a substitute. Before she reached the van she had been plied with sandwiches, scones and two cups of tea. She entered the van with relief, depositing her fare on the bench.

'Can you use these?' she asked. It was a different co-ordinator from last night.

'No fear.' He grinned. 'I'm not game to put my nose out the van door for fear of getting another scone! If the boys don't report in soon I'm going to start offending people.'

Joanne smiled perfunctorily. 'No word?'

'Nothing.' He frowned at her as she lowered herself stiffly into a sitting position. 'Are you all right?'

'Fine,' Joanne lied. 'Just a bit stiff after yesterday.'

'Yes, I heard about that. You've had quite a weekend, all in all.'

'It's not over yet,' she reminded him. 'We've got one little boy to find before it's over.'

'That means we have to find him today.'

'That's right.' She looked at him steadily. 'Where's Cam?'

'Mr Maddon?' The policeman sighed. 'He's out with a party again. We tried to persuade him to stay here in case the boy's found, but he can't stay still.'

'He's been up all night?'

The policeman nodded.

'And Mrs Maddon?'

'I can tell you that.' A police car had pulled up beside the van while they were talking and the island's senior officer entered. 'She's gone.'

'Gone?'

'Done a bunk,' the man said crudely. 'Those friends of hers she spent the day with yesterday upped anchor this morning. According to the hotel staff, Mrs Maddon checked out and left with them, luggage and all.'

For a moment there was silence. Joanne found that her nails were clenching and unclenching into claws. How could Lindy do it? How could she go and just leave them? The young officer policeman shook his head.

'Why on earth?'

The older man shook his head grimly. 'She's not my idea of a motherly type, that's for certain. When we discovered she'd been lying to us about when the boy had been last seen yesterday I warned her of a possible charge of child neglect. I doubt if it'd stick, but I was trying to make her see the gravity of her actions. The fact that her son is missing didn't seem to be all that important to her. The possibility of legal action against her had much more effect. I guess she took fright.'

Joanne nodded silently. Her initial summing-up of Lindy had been horribly correct.

She left the van and sat on the same log that Cam had used yesterday, waiting for the searchers to return. Periodically one of the women of the auxiliary would approach her with a cup of tea, but for the most part she was left alone. The hospital knew where she was, but there were no calls. Sunday was usually a quiet day, and by now the entire island would know that the doctor's son was missing.

Towards midday Cam returned. He was still with a group of men, but before they came individually into view Joanne could pick him out. His shoulders were slumped and he staggered as he walked. Another of the men had him by the arm. He looked gratefully up as Joanne approached.

'I'm glad you're here, Doc.' He gestured to Cam. 'He's been with us since dawn and he was with another group all night. He's been driving himself harder than the rest of us put together. He was all right until we suggested having a break, then he just seemed to lose his grip, got really angry and. . .well, you can see.'

Joanne nodded. Cam was concentrating on putting one foot in front of another. He was past even acknowledging Joanne's presence. 'Bring him into the van, will you, and can someone fetch my bag from the back of the car?'

Cam didn't speak as Joanne pulled his boots off and

she and her helper lowered him on to a bunk. He had pushed himself past the limits of exhaustion. He made no protest as Joanne put a sleeping-tablet in his mouth and watched as he swallowed it.

'He'll sleep without it,' she explained to the man helping her, 'but it'll stop him waking up in half an hour, wanting to go again.' She put a hand up on the side of his face and ran it lightly down his cheek. He was already asleep. She turned to the police chief. 'He's not to go out again, even if you have to chain him here. It's going to kill him, but otherwise he's going to kill himself. He's past being rational.'

The radio in the corner crackled to life. Joanne was wanted at the hospital again.

When she returned late that evening Cam was awake. He was seated on his log, drinking tea from a big tin mug. Joanne thought back to the well-groomed man of forty-eight hours ago and grimaced. He was still wearing the clothes he'd had on when he was called from the hospital yesterday. Once they'd been well-tailored trousers and a casual shirt. Now they were ripped and stained beyond recognition. A day's dark stubble was on his chin. He looked like something off a 'wanted' poster, Joanne thought grimly. Even the haunted expression in his eyes was right.

'Love?' She hadn't meant to say it. The word had been torn out of her. He looked up at her and she went to him.

She held him as she would a hurt and frightened child, crooning, rocking, making nonsense noises of reassurance. At first he was rigid, tense against her, but she kept her hold. Her fingers moved through the dark hair, holding his unshaven face against her.

Gradually the rigidity lessened, and she felt him

relax into her. Every now and then a shudder would run through his frame. She moved her hands around to touch his face and realised there were tears on his cheeks. She stayed silent. He had to release the dreadful tension somehow.

Finally it was over. The shudders lessened and then stopped. He pulled back and looked at her.

'Jo?'

'Mmm?'

He ran a hand through her hair and pulled her face down on to his chest. 'I do love you.'

'I know.'

'Mind you,' he continued unsteadily, 'my judgement of women is a bit suspect.'

She pulled back. 'Cam Maddon, if you once compare me to that. . .that. . .' Words failed her. 'Do you know what she's done?'

'Left the island? Yes, the police told me when I woke up. You did warn me about her.'

'You knew yourself.'

'Yes,' he admitted tiredly. 'I just kept trying to do what I'd done all along, ascribe to her values she never really had. I just can't believe she's really Tom's mother.'

'She's not,' Joanne said firmly. 'Her behaviour this weekend has lost her any claim she might have had to the title.'

'Well.' He looked at her and smiled faintly through the grime. 'He's going to need a new one, then.'

'Is this a proposal?'

'I seem to remember I've already made you one of those.' He broke off at the sound of a returning party. Nothing.

'I'm kidding myself,' he said sadly. 'Tom wouldn't

have gone into the bush. Why the hell would he? The only logical explanation is that he got into trouble in the water and no one was around to pull him out. That's what all these guys think, but they're just too kind to say so.'

'They're making a pretty good show of searching for men who don't believe they'll find something,' Joanne said stoutly. 'Cam, I'm about to issue orders, so don't interrupt.'

'No, ma'am.'

She looked up at him suspiciously, but there was no hint of a smile.

'I'm taking you back to the hospital for a shower, a shave and to collect a change of clothes for the morning.' She held up a hand as he made to interrupt. 'I know—your place is here. I'll bring you back here to sleep and I'll leave you only after I've watched you swallow another sleeping-pill. You are no use to anyone in the state you were in at lunchtime.'

'No, ma'am.'

'No arguments?'

'I know when it's useless to fight. Dr Tynon with her mind made up is a force to be reckoned with.' He stopped and put his hand under her chin. 'Joanne, are you OK yourself? You look awful.'

'What a charming thing to say,' she grimaced at him.

'Is something wrong?'

Her back was on fire with pain radiating down into her leg, but this was certainly not the time to admit it. 'Nothing that won't be cured by finding Tom,' she said lightly.

At three the next morning Joanne gave up the effort to sleep. Each slight movement would start the driving shafts of pain shooting downward. She had taken as much painkiller as she dared, but it wasn't much. There were patients in the hospital who depended on her. Having drugged Cam, she could hardly do the same to herself. If Tom was not found the following day she was going to have to call on Cairns for an emergency doctor, she thought. If she were her own patient she would insist on a week's bed rest until the bruising around her spine had subsided.

She either had to lie or stand; sitting was unbearable. Towards dawn she abandoned bed and went to find the night sister.

'I'm going for a walk down to the beach. I won't go far. Send someone down if you need me.'

'But it's still dark!'

Joanne gestured outside to where the first glimmer of dawn was showing. 'By the time I get to the beach it will be morning.'

'Doctor?'

'Yes.'

'Are you all right? Is it my imagination, or are you walking stiffly?'

'I'm fine,' Joanne snapped, then caught herself. 'I'm sorry—I'm just a bit tense.'

'Aren't we all?' the girl agreed quietly. 'Two nights he's been out there now.'

Joanne bit her lip and turned away.

The beach was strangely unfamiliar in the dim light. Joanne stretched out full length on the sand, trying to ease the gnawing in her back and leg. It wouldn't fade.

The sea was as calm as she had ever seen it. Tiny ripples murmured in rhythm, but apart from that there was no sound.

It was hard to say when Joanne first heard it. It wasn't so much a sound as a break of the stillness. She lay motionless, trying to make it out.

It came again, a trace of echo carried across the water. Before it ended Joanne was on her feet, yelling as if her life depended on it.

'Tom? Tom, are you there? Tom, can you hear me?'

There was an awful silence and then a sobbing cry, and Joanne knew she was right.

Where was he? Joanne was running towards the end of the little cove, knowing before she reached the jutting outcrop of rock that he wasn't on this side. As she neared the rock barrier she called again.

'Tom?'

There was a response, faint but sure. A glorious flood of sureness flooded through her. It had to be him.

But how to get to him? The rock jutted far out to sea. The obvious answer was to go back to the hospital and get men to bash their way through the bush to where he was. As far as she knew there was no track down. Or perhaps a boat? Even as she thought of them she was rejecting both these options. Tom had heard her—she was sure of that. If she left now and it took half an hour to fetch help, what would Tom do? She looked up at the jagged rock-face and shuddered. If he tried to climb. . .

'Tom?' She stopped and listened. There was no response. Perhaps even now he was starting to climb.

Joanne hauled off her jeans and windcheater and spread them out on the sand. Grabbing a stick, she dragged it through the sand, making a huge arrow to the rock face. There was no time for more. Within seconds she was in the water, swimming steadily out to round the cliff.

She hadn't reckoned on her back. Every arm-stroke hurt, and after the first couple of kicks she simply let her legs hang uselessly behind her. It was agonising to do anything else.

The water was deep and dark, the dawn not yet far enough advanced to transform it to its usual brilliant green. It was a different feeling, swimming in the half-light. Things brushed against her skin as she swam. Weed, she hoped. She daren't let herself believe it was anything else.

As she neared the point the swell rose. The current was doing its best to pull her back from the way she wanted to go. For a moment she let fear poke its greasy tentacles into her mind. She was being carried out. She blotted out the pain in her back and kicked. It was bad, but the fear of drowning was worse.

Then she was around. On the other side of the outcrop the water was still exposed, but at least the current had eased. She put her head down and went for the shore.

He had already started to climb. The first thing Joanne thought when she saw him was, Thank God I came. He had started to climb striaght up a rock-face that loomed above them for thirty feet. He was ten feet up, but had obviously heard her coming and stopped.

How Joanne got him down she never afterwards remembered. Somehow she reached him and somehow they were on the beach together, with Tom dissolved into a bundle of sobbing joy in her fierce hold.

It was nearly midday before Cam found them.

For Joanne the swim had been the last effort she was

capable of making. She lay on the sand, holding Tom close, drawing as much comfort from him as he did from her.

He wasn't hurt. His body was a mass of scratches and bruises and he was dragging his bad leg, but apart from that his two nights in the open seemed to have done little damage. Whatever he had been through could wait until later to be told. He was content now to lie close.

It was just as well. Joanne's head was light with dizziness as the pain in her back threatened to overcome her. She lay very still, willing Tom to do the same.

'Where's my dad?' he asked drowsily, after a little while.

'He'll come,' Joanne murmured confidently.

'How will he know we're here?'

'I left him a message.'

'Oh.' He assimilated this and found it satisfactory. 'I'm thirsty. Do you think he'll be here soon?'

'Soon.'

It was enough. Tom drifted into sleep.

For the rest of the morning they lay unmoving on the beach. At some stage Joanne was dimly aware of distant shouting from the other side of the cove, but it was beyond her to rise and shout back. Finally there was the unmistakable noise of a motorboat approaching. She pushed her head up to see, but pain sheared through her like a knife. She lay back, the child's body warm against her skin. There was the sound of the boat being beached, shouting and running feet. Through a swirling mist of pain there was Cam, bent over to hold the two figures close. Then nothing.

CHAPTER THIRTEEN

JOANNE woke to sunlight pouring in through a big french window. The window was open, allowing the soft curtains to move gently in the breeze. She opened her eyes wide in puzzlement. It was familiar, and yet. . . Where was she?

Hospital. She was in one of the private rooms at the hospital. She tried to move her head to take in her surroundings but the effort was too much. She closed her eyes and waited.

There were footsteps, the sure tread she knew so well. He was here. His fingers gently traced the contours of her face, and she opened her eyes to see her love reflected in his gaze.

'Cam.' It was a thready whisper.

'Hush.' His finger gently closed her lips. 'You're to do nothing but sleep.'

'Tom?' She fought against his lips to form the word.

'Is fine. Thanks to you, my love. He'd been in the bush until yesterday afternoon and managed to find some fresh water, so he's not even badly dehydrated.' Cam stopped and took Joanne's limp hand in his. 'He had some luck when he reached the point where you found him, though. If he'd tried to get round that himself. . .' He looked down at her, then bent and kissed her gently on the lips.

'And now, sleep, my own Joanne. Sleep.'

She did. When next she woke it was dark and a nurse

was sitting beside her bed. The room focused and cleared.

'Well, I was beginning to think Mr Maddon had overdosed you,' the nurse smiled. 'Welcome back.' She proffered a glass with bent straw attached. 'Would you like a drink?'

'Mmm.' She took a sip. 'No pillows?'

'Flat on your back for however long it takes,' the girl said firmly. 'If you argue I have orders to tie you down.'

'So who's arguing?' The relief to be rid of the shooting pain was unbelievable. Joanne guessed that Cam had administered morphine. That and the rigidity of the firm, flat bed held the pain in abeyance. She smiled. 'Tom is all right?'

'Tucked up in his own bed. I've been in to check for myself—as has every other member of the hospital. He's a bit peeved because we wouldn't let him in here to visit.'

Joanne moved her head cautiously. No pain. Tentatively she tried to wriggle her toes. Her left foot was numb.

'I wouldn't bother with any more testing,' the nurse said, amused. 'Mr Maddon thinks it's a disc lesion.'

'Sciatica,' Cam's voice agreed with her from the doorway. 'Thanks, Sister.' He nodded dismissal to the nurse and crossed to the bed. 'We'll do an X-ray later to be on the safe side. If you'd gone to bed for twenty-four hours after it happened you wouldn't be in this mess.'

'I don't see that I had much choice,' she said defensively. 'Who was going to deliver Mrs Neilson if I didn't?'

'Or do all the routine work, plus look after me, plus

swim half a mile in the open sea to save my son from falling to his death. Who else indeed?' He sat down on the bed beside her and took her face tenderly between his hands. 'My lovely Jo.' He ran a finger down to the tip of her nose. 'Can you imagine how I felt this morning to be given a message that you'd been at the beach since dawn and they couldn't find you? They'd only found your clothes.'

'But I left an arrow!' Joanne cringed at what he'd obviously thought.

'As I found when I got to the beach. It was one hell of a drive before I got there, though. I thought I'd lost you both.'

'Oh, Cam!'

'Oh, Joanne,' he mimicked her fondly. 'From here on you and Tom are both going to be kept well and truly under lock and key. I'll let you out for exercise once a week on the front lawn of the hospital.'

'Yes, sir,' she said meekly.

He looked down at her. Their eyes held them together, each giving and receiving affirmation of their love.

'Does this mean you won't be going to England, then?' Joanne asked unsteadily.

'I would love to take you to England,' Cam said seriously. 'But it'll have to wait until Lindy hits the big lights of Hollywood. I'm not letting Tom within a thousand miles of her.'

Joanne smiled sadly. 'I don't really see that happening, do you? I can't see Lindy making a success of her life, on any terms.'

'Do you feel sorry for her?' As Joanne nodded Cam shook his head incredulously. 'Perhaps I'll come to it in time, but at the moment she's nearly cost me all I hold precious in the world. Enough.' He stood up. 'You have some solid sleeping to do, my girl. You have a wedding to be fit for. How about a month on Saturday?'

'A whole month!'

'It can't be done sooner. I checked.'

Joanne smiled drowsily. 'It sounds good to me.' The drugs were taking hold again and she was drifting off on a tide of contentment. 'Will Tom approve?'

'The only person who's going to be happier than Tom,' Cam said decisively, bending to kiss her lightly on the lips, 'is Tom Maddon's father.'

CHAPTER FOURTEEN

AT THE bottom of Joanne's suitcase lay a parcel, neatly wrapped with white tissue paper. It had lain there for two months, since Joanne had tossed it there in laughing disbelief after her shopping trip with Barbara all that time ago. Not so long ago. Joanne shook her head in disbelief at how her life had been transformed.

'Joanne Maddon.' She rolled it around her tongue. It sounded strange.

Strange but true. On the third finger of Joanne's left hand lay a bright circlet of gold. The marriage had taken place this morning, under the giant trees of the hospital garden, followed by a party attended by nearly every inhabitant of Strathleath. And the rest. Barbara and Wayne had been there with their baby son and William with his lady. And Tom. Joanne smiled at the memory of the little boy lording it over the ceremony.

'It was my idea,' he had told everyone proudly. 'I thought of it.'

He had been a little disgusted at being left behind on the honeymoon, but Barbara took a hand. She'd explained that they needed Tom to help care for the baby as she and Wayne looked after the hospital. Permission had been grudgingly granted. Besides, if a honeymoon was necessary in order to get this thing tied up—well, Tom wouldn't stand in its way.

The house Cam had brought Joanne to was on the mainland, a short charter flight from Strathleath. Its beauty was its isolation. No phone, no patients, nobody. Perched high on a rugged headland overlooking the ocean, from the balcony you could see forever. Cam was out there now, watching the sea as Joanne showered and unpacked her tissue parcel.

She came out shyly. For a month they had hardly been near each other, each holding back for this, their final commitment.

Cam turned as she approached. She stopped, waiting. The wind caught her hair, tossing it around her face. The soft white folds of the nightgown swirled around her.

Slowly he came towards her, his face a mixture of pride and love.

'Did I ever say I didn't want you to wear lovely clothes?' His hands came out to hold her at arm's length. 'I must have been mad.'

'Cam?' Her voice was a breathless whisper. The breeze was blowing the dark hair back from his face, flattening his silk shirt against his chest. She loved him so much she couldn't bear it.

'Yes?'

'Nothing,' she faltered. Her fingers moved up to touch his beloved face.

His eyes understood. Slowly he slipped the outer wrap from her shoulders and let it fall. The breeze flattened the sheer cotton to her body. It was warm and caressing, holding her in thrall.

Then they were in each other's arms and Joanne was being lifted and carried inside to where the bed lay waiting. The exquisite nightgown somehow disappeared, to become a crumpled heap of soft white fabric on the floor. What Joanne had suspected all along became proven fact. She didn't really need it.

Life and death drama in this gripping new novel of passion and suspense

Following a vicious attack on a tough property developer and his beautiful wife, eminent surgeon David Compton fought fiercely to save both lives, little knowing just how deeply he would become involved in a complex web of deadly revenge. Ginette Irving, the cool and practical theatre sister, was an enigma to David, but could he risk an affair with the worrying threat to his career and now the sinister attempts on his life?

W**O**RLDWIDE

Price: £3.99   Published: May 1991

Available from Boots, Martins, John Menzies, W.H. Smith, Woolworths and other paperback stockists.

Also available from Mills and Boon Reader Service, P.O. Box 236, Thornton Road, Croydon, Surrey CR9 3RU

Mills & Boon

Discover the thrill of 4 Exciting Medical Romances – FREE

FREE

BOOKS FOR YOU

In the exciting world of modern medicine, the emotions of true love have an added drama. Now you can experience four of these unforgettable romantic tales of passion and heartbreak FREE – and look forward to a regular supply of Mills & Boon Medical Romances delivered direct to your door!

❧ ❧ ❧

Turn the page for details of 2 extra free gifts, and how to apply.

An Irresistible Offer from Mills & Boon

Here's an offer from Mills & Boon to become a regular reader of Medical Romances. To welcome you, we'd like you to have four books, a cuddly teddy and a special MYSTERY GIFT, all absolutely free and without obligation.

Then, every month you could look forward to receiving 4 more **brand new** Medical Romances for £1.45 each, delivered direct to your door, post and packing free. Plus our newsletter featuring author news, competitions, special offers, and lots more.

This invitation comes with no strings attached. You can cancel or suspend your subscription at any time, and still keep your free books and gifts.

Its so easy. Send no money now. Simply fill in the coupon below and post it at once to -

Mills & Boon Reader Service, FREEPOST, PO Box 236, Croydon, Surrey CR9 9EL

NO STAMP REQUIRED

YES! Please rush me my 4 Free Medical Romances and 2 Free Gifts! Please also reserve me a Reader Service Subscription. If I decide to subscribe, I can look forward to receiving 4 brand new Medical Romances every month for just £5.80, delivered direct to my door. Post and packing is free, and there's a free Mills & Boon Newsletter. If I choose not to subscribe I shall write to you within 10 days - I can keep the books and gifts whatever I decide. I can cancel or suspend my subscription at any time. I am over 18.

EP03D

Name (Mr/Mrs/Ms) _____

Address _____

_____

_____ Postcode _____

Signature _____

The right is reserved to refuse an application and change the terms of this offer. Offer expires **July 31st 1991**. Readers in Southern Africa write to P.O. Box 2125, Randburg, South Africa. Other Overseas and Eire, send for details. You may be mailed with other offers from Mills & Boon and other reputable companies as a result of this application. If you would prefer not to share in this opportunity, please tick box. ☐